BIG CITY GOTH GF

KIRK MASON

Copyright © 2024 by Kirk Mason

All rights reserved.

No part of this book may be reproduced in any form or by any electronic or mechanical means, including information storage and retrieval systems, without written permission from the author, except for the use of brief quotations in a book review.

You can contact me at: kirkmasonbooks@gmail.com

CHAPTER ONE

MICHAEL

"Watch out!" Michael yelled.

Boulders crashed amidst the ruins. Stone dust billowed, stinging his eyes. The soot blanketed the golden statue of Lady Rathe, the cat god, and what was once a shining splendor was now a dim, dusty gray. However, the emerald eyes continued to sparkle.

"Sorry!" Tommy said, a scruffy-haired kid wearing expensive sneakers.

Michael's nephew was a good kid, but a bad explorer. Michael had felt good about taking him under his wing, despite his best instincts, and now his instincts screamed to get the guy out of there. Tommy had butterfingers, jelly for legs, and feet that turned every surface he stepped on to ice.

"Pass that over," Michael said, holding his hand

out for the bag. The lack of patience began to show in his voice. He'd held it back for as long as he could.

"Sorry," Tommy said again, averting his gaze.

"Just watch where you're going." Michael tried to steady his voice, hearing it as it echoed in the empty cavern. He'd been molded by tough teachers growing up. Sometimes, too tough. He didn't want to be like them, but perhaps he'd have to be.

Michael sighed, surveying the area.

Long, red flags draped down the cavernous depths. Black-tailed demons in the center spoke of a long-dead sect of the catkin empire. Rocks from Tommy's slip-up still trailed down the steps they'd just descended.

But it was fine. It was just rocks. Nothing to worry about.

Michael gripped the heavy bag in his hands and stared cautiously at the ancient artifact before the statue of the cat god. *Only a fool would try this*, Michael thought, exactly as they'd expect of him. Replace the item with another, like something from a movie.

Some people thought Lady Rathe's golden crown belonged in a museum. Maybe that could have been Michael's path one day, finding artifacts for museums. But his uncle paid better to have it in his shop. Besides, most museums these days were wary of being accused of 'stealing the relics of another culture.'

Ol' Uncle Patrick held no such cares. And besides, this ancient kingdom of evil demon cats was long gone. Their armies were vanquished by humans long ago, and the catkin now wandering around the realm didn't act like they did.

All that was left was to take the spoils.

"Want me to—" Tommy began.

"Just keep holding the light," Michael said. Sweat clung his shirt to his back. The dust seemed to scrape against his flesh.

"Sure thing, Mikey."

"Just call me Michael." Michael slowly pulled the crown and read the words upon his scroll in ancient demonic. "*Raadaa, zee naa dee, teell fa—*"

"Sounds a bit funny, that," Tommy chimed, interrupting him.

"Damn it!"

The earth shook beneath his feet. The emeralds of Lady Rathe's eyes glowed a bright red.

Emeralds glowing red was usually not a good sign.

He yanked the kid's arm. "Run!" he said, and they paced up the steps three at a time. The kid was fast, at least. Michael let go of his arm as they ran up the steps.

Ancient skeletons rose from their more ancient slumbers, blades of rusty steel in their eternal grips.

Tommy dodged the swing of one, leaped over a fallen pillar, and ducked just in time for an arrow to fly over him. Michael did the same and thought it some cruel mercy that the kid was there to alert him to the danger.

"Piss off," Michael said to a skeleton, punching it in the jaw, shattering the bones.

It hurt his knuckles, but it must've hurt the skeleton more because it shattered to the ground in pieces. Old necromancy tended to lose its potency after several thousand years.

Traps did not.

"Remember the trick platform!" Michael yelled.

"Got it!" Tommy leaped over the thing way too far, skidding onto the ground. A draugr stood over him, blue eyes glimmering at its fallen prey.

The blade raised high, and Michael pulled his gun from his holster, cocked the hammer, and shot right through the skull of the thing, sending it flying back to whatever hells from which it had spawned.

Michael arrived at the narrow tunnel, where Tommy was trying to lift himself, yelping in pain.

"Twisted my—" Tommy began.

Michael threw the lanky kid over his shoulder, grunting from the weight as he continued his run. The jingling sound of bones followed them, the caves around them shook, and Michael decided never to do a favor for a relative again. His damn brother's words echoed in his mind. *'He's a good kid. Just give him a chance.'*

Kids can be good and dumb at the same time, Michael thought, as guilt raged in him, knowing that he had been given a chance once, too. No longer, no more chances. Michael didn't need a partner, he didn't need an apprentice. He needed to get in and get out as he'd always done.

A tiny dot of light sparkled in the distance. Poor Tommy's twisted ankle smacked against his thigh, and the kid screamed in anguish. An arrow shot for them. Michael threw himself against the wall as it whooshed past them to land into an approaching skeleton that was just seconds away from swiping at them.

Michael took a second and a deep breath, and then he ran for the exit. His shoulder ached, but adrenaline pumped through him, sending the pain to the back of his mind.

A cutting, slicing feeling shot through his calf. He looked down in horror as an arrow jutted through his trousers, and he crashed to the ground, the arrow snapping off as he fell.

He crawled, bloody fingers digging into the dirt, until finally, he touched grass, and he rolled onto his back to the bright sun.

"That was crazy!" Tommy exclaimed, falling beside him. "Gods, my ankle is killing me."

The boulders crashed over the mountain entrance, swallowed by the mountain until it was closed. The contents would be forgotten by history. The maps, the ancient language, were all lost now. Ol' Uncle Patrick was staunch against putting any of his findings on the internet.

"Tommy," Michael said with a painful sigh. "You're fired."

"Fair enough," Tommy replied. "Holy...your leg!"

Spots of purple dotted Michael's vision. "On second thought, you're not fired yet. Fancy calling me an ambulance?"

SERENA

The knight's helmet dropped to the floor, clanging and crashing with ear-piercing thunder. The two men in the store jumped in surprise and rushed to help her.

She glanced behind her, down the hallway leading to Patrick's office. At any moment, he would poke his head out the doorway to see what the commotion was.

Yet, he did not. She heard him turn the page of his newspaper.

"Stupid drow," he mumbled, yet loud enough for her to hear. She heard him turn another page. "What did you drop this time?" he yelled.

"The Helmet of Hubert the Hero," Serena said. "That one wasn't expensive, was it?"

"Expensive? Expensive! It's priceless! He slayed a thousand of your kind. A hero if there ever was one. Be more careful, won't you?"

"I can't promise anything!" Serena sang. She then grunted in frustration, and was soon distracted by the customer walking towards the counter.

"Here," he said, holding out the helmet. "I'm sure it will buff out."

A huge dent had formed in the helmet. Serena gasped in joy and grabbed the helmet, then rushed to the back room to show it proudly to Patrick.

The gray-haired antique salesman peered up from his glasses, raising his bushy eyebrows.

Serena held it more proudly, thrusting it towards him. "I broke it," she said with a beaming smile.

Patrick shook his head. "Another one? One might think you're doing it on purpose."

"Imagine that," Serena said. "You'd almost think I was trying to get fired." *Hint hint.*

"You wouldn't do that, then you'd be some deadbeat sucking off the court's teet. No, my dear, you've got a stable job here and should count yourself lucky."

Serena huffed as rage came over her.

She was vaguely lucky, in some loose sense of the word. A drow could not get employment in the human realm. Serena was half-drow. The light lilac hue of her skin and slightly smaller pointed ears made that painfully obvious to her and other drow. But to humans, she was just another sneaky moon elf.

Nobody wanted to hire a drow. Folk thought them evil incarnate.

Many centuries had passed since all the great wars, and most races lived in harmony. Even goblins seemed to get a good rep these days—mostly because of how compatible the short-stack females were with human males.

But drow?

Nobody liked drow, even if it was against the law to admit it. Even when she went to the bookstore, the romance section barely stocked any drow smut, and what was there just gathered dust.

Goblin girls? Those books sold like hotcakes. It seemed like men couldn't get enough of them. When the hell would people get sick of goblin girls and move on to some other fascination, like slimes?

Serena wished she was a slime so that she could sink into the ground and never be seen again.

"If I thought you were trying to get fired," Patrick said, "I'd only be more lenient on you."

Patrick liked drow the least. Yet, he'd seen fit not to mention that when hiring her.

Finally, she'd thought, at their interview. *A nice old man who'd let me sit on the counter and read books all day.*

Instead, she was subjected to countless history lessons about how evil her people were—all the atrocities they'd committed in the name of the Night God.

She'd been specifically made to polish, over and over, any artifact that had been involved in the drow wars. He made a habit of it, grinning as he watched her. At first, she thought he was just letching on her like an old pervert.

He just liked making her look the Helmet of Hubert in the eye holes.

It wasn't *her* fault her people used to be evil! *And could probably still be if one compares their laws to humans.* Still, why did goblins get a free pass? Because of their juicy, scrumptious, delicious goblin pussies. Obviously.

Serena huffed and returned to the counter, hoping one of the customers had decided to steal something. Instead, he patiently awaited her, with his selection of potions ready to be paid for.

The glowing red and blue vials gave off a faint mana hum. Serena packed them into a plastic bag, resisted the urge to drop them, and then wished the man a nice day.

"You too," he said, giving her a warm smile.

See, she thought, *not everyone hates me.*

Her pointy ear tickled as Patrick grunted, leaving his office. He hobbled over past the counter, placing his hands on his hips as he surveyed the shop.

"Needs another clean," he said.

"I just cleaned it an hour ago," Serena replied.

"These artifacts, they're important. And the potions are gathering dust already!" He gave her a wicked grin.

Serena huffed and walked over, her Dick Marvin boots stomping on the ground as she grabbed the folded-up stepladder, undid it, and climbed up to the potion rack. These were their best sellers. Most people these days did not have the spare cash to buy useless artifacts, but everyone needed potions. Mana, health, virility. Some of them were real, most of them were diluted.

She ran the duster over their glimmering crystal while Patrick watched over her, ensuring she got every spec. Then, she unlocked the cabinet full of dangerous potions. One held a black liquid, a void in which the dim orange light of the shop got sucked into, never to be seen again.

"Be careful with that one!" he said.

"I am very careful!" she yelled, with fury in her crimson eyes. "I told you about this one myself." When she turned, her hand slipped, but she caught herself.

"Watch it!" Patrick grabbed the stepladder to steady her. She slipped again from disgust at his hand being near her foot, this time missing the edge and brushing past the ebony potion of her homeland. The crystal bottle slipped off the ledge and smashed into the ground, making her wince. Vapor wafted upwards as it swam into Patrick's hairy nostrils and he fainted, smashing his head on the edge of the stepladder.

Serena blinked in disbelief. The poison potion met her nostrils, where it harmlessly ran through her bloodstream, thanks to her race's immunity to a potion made from mushrooms found in their realm.

"That one was *actually* an accident," she said, blinking as she stared at him. "You're not dead, are you?"

He snorted as some horrid liquid pooled out the back of his head.

CHAPTER
TWO

MICHAEL

"Nearly done," the kindly bunnykin cleric said. Her white overcoat was adorable against the pink of her hair and white ears. She murmured words of power as mana coated Michael's shin, dispelling the wound to make the flesh of his skin as pink as her hair.

The hospital ward had this holy air about the place. A shrine to the God of Healing hummed away at the back, and nurses and doctors stood over a hexray in the corner, discussing what may be wrong with a patient. One of them mentioned his lungs had been sent to another dimension, yet still functioning perfectly well via the two portals in his body. They planned to operate on him and pull the lungs back from whatever realm they'd trotted off to.

Michael's phone rang, and he fished it out of his

pocket. He frowned at the number, not recognizing it. At first, he did not want to answer. Anything important would have resulted in a voicemail soon after. But he still had a few hours left in the hospital while they ran tests to check if the magic had taken correctly, so he pressed the green button.

"Michael Walker?" the voice asked. "I have you down as Patrick Walker's next of kin."

Michael sat up. "Is he okay?" he asked.

"I'm afraid he's in the hospital," she said down the line.

That makes two of us, Michael thought.

"He's stable for the moment," the doctor explained. "He's ingested some kind of drow potion our clerics haven't seen before, but a drow is flying over. We did manage to converge with Patrick telepathically for a moment before he was lost to the poison stasis. He requested you look after his shop in lieu of coming to see him."

"Look after his..." Michael frowned. "Sure he doesn't want me to visit him?"

What the hell was Michael supposed to do in a shop? Sit and count change? He'd briefly worked retail as a teen, but that was in some liquor store. He didn't know the first thing about running his uncle's place, regardless of how many items he'd delivered there.

A twinge of guilt shot up his spine. That very potion that had got him was one *he'd* collected from an incredibly rare drow tomb in the human realm. A highly illegal expedition. Their people would be furious if word got out, and it sounded like it had.

The cleric tending to his leg appeared to have been listening to his conversation, as she said, "You can't do anything strenuous for at least a few weeks."

Michael nodded. "I'll head over there in a few hours," he said on the phone.

"I must remind you I can't relay this message to him. Our ability to make contact has ceased."

"Right, right, sure." Michael swung his legs off the bed.

The bunnykin cleric looked up from her notes and scowled, "Sir, you must wait!"

Michael stood up, flexing his legs. "It worked," he said. "There's no need for protocol, but I promise I'll take it easy."

˜

The *Relics of Wonder* sign swung gently in a breeze. Below, the display was filled with fascinating artifacts. The sword with the emerald gem first caught his eye. It lay flat across the bottom, like a frame for the rest of the items.

He thought back to his past, evacuating a tomb where he found a statue that'd given him pause—a mothkin and her knight, hugging together, carved in stone, the sword rested at their feet. He'd looked into the story once. Apparently, they had both lived to be ancient, finally succumbing to death but weeks from one another after many happy decades of ruling from their manor.

Above were gauntlets, helmets, and many typical old knights' stuff anyone could buy on the internet. However, there was one glowing amethyst infused with some kind of lightning mana, sparkling inside it.

Michael had nearly blown his hand off finding that one. He looked at the price Patrick was selling it for and whistled. His uncle was making a killing off his discoveries.

He frowned. Music was playing from the store—pop music, pumping drums. He'd thought the store was empty. He squinted inside and couldn't see anything through the gaps in the display but more shelving obscuring the view.

Michael headed to the door and slotted his key in, and found it already unlocked.

When he opened the door, a crash of music overcame him like a thunder blast. Rising above it was the most off-tune, impassioned singing he'd ever heard. It sounded like something was dying yet refusing to with glee.

'Working eight to six, what a shitty way to make barely-a living!' the banshee cried. *'Getting paid like crap for the crap my boss is giving.'*

Michael traversed through the towering shelves of robes, skulls, and chests. The potion shelves chimed from the vibration of her wailing. Michael's heart raced. He felt like he was walking through a dangerous tomb.

Finally, he broke through the labyrinth to see a lilac woman with her bare feet on the table. She wore fishnet stockings, and her cute toes poked through the rips, flexing as she sang. Her fingers were locked over her stomach, and above this, a lusciously swollen set of tits were compressed so tight in a black crop top corset, they looked ready to pop. Her belly poked out from underneath—a tiny bit chubby, in a cute way.

Her eyes were closed behind her glasses, though the snarl on her black-painted lips, as she sang, suggested she might be ready to throw a few expletives Michael's way if he interrupted her *Greenhaven's Got Talent* audition.

He inspected her more. With her fishnet sleeves over her corset crop top, she didn't look like the sort of person to like this singer. But hells, everyone liked this song, even if they didn't want to admit it.

"Great singing," Michael said. "I'm not sure I approve of the new lyrics. It ain't right to mess with the classics."

The drow opened her eyes, and violent crimson orbs stared at him in shock. She hurried to get her feet off the counter and tidy herself up, brushing something off her unseen legs—crumbs, perhaps, judging from the half-empty packet on the counter.

"Announce yourself before you sneak up on people!" she snapped.

"Great customer service, too. I can see why my uncle hired you."

"You're..." Her nose twitched, and then she swallowed, her neck flexing hypnotically. She leaned over the counter, and a spiky heart necklace clanged on the glass. "You're Michael," she said. "That guy who dives into tombs." She gave a challenging squint.

"Guilty," Michael replied. "My uncle asked me to come look after his shop. Didn't mention I didn't have to, though, because you're here."

She crossed her arms tighter, staring at him. She had a cute nose, less angular and pointy than many drow's he'd seen. Judging from the paleness of her skin, she was not fully drow. Her ears weren't as long either, though were still plenty pointy.

"I've only been here a month," she said.

"Makes sense. I've not spoken to him in two. Been away on a long expedition."

"Steal anything good?"

"Got injured actually, was just in the hospital myself."

"Serves—" she began, then cut herself off. "Well, at least you're fine now. How is Patrick?"

"In stasis."

"Like I left him, then."

What was her problem? Michael sighed, then walked over to the counter. She tensed up as he opened the hatch.

"I'll be in the back room," he said. "Catching up with paperwork, or whatever it is he does here."

"And I'll be here," she said, then turned the dial of the music. A violent metal guitar rang out. More fitting and appropriate to her attire.

Michael returned to the counter, leaned over, and turned the dial down. "Let's keep it a little more of a friendly volume," he said.

"Fine," she replied. Her lips tightened for a second, then she held her hand out, perhaps finally realizing how awfully she'd been acting. "My name is Serena," she said.

"Michael." They shook hands. Her fingers felt soft against his, though she gripped with elven strength that could have crushed his bones.

"I know, you told me," she replied.

"Nope, *you* told me," Michael grinned. "Remember?"

She squinted.

Note to self—the drow has zero sense of humor. Or you're just not very funny. Maybe both.

~

SERENA

Serena huffed, crossing her arms and sitting back in the chair. It was bullshit. She was supposed to have the shop to herself for an entire week. It was a holiday she was getting paid for! She could have read books, she could have played her music, she could have diddled herself something silly in the bathroom.

And now, she was to battle a younger, more virile monster than the old dragon she'd been fighting. What new tricks did this newer model have up his sleeve? He'd feigned politeness on entry. Anyone related to that monster had to be cut from the same cloth.

She dug into her packet of crisps, enjoying the lovely salty vinegar taste. Her mother always said she shouldn't eat these. They'd make her put on weight. She patted her ever-so-pudgy belly. *Now I'm gonna eat them even harder!* she thought. *Just to spite you.* What did her father ever see in her mother?

What did anyone ever see in anyone?

She got up, put her hands behind her back, and strolled around the shop to the book section. There was a selection of knights' tales, some about the heroes of old, and one about the history of King's Knights.

She doubted that such silliness existed. The sword outside was likely fake. You could never tell what was fake and real in this place. It was a travesty. An insult to the great histories of their time!

'I love history,' she'd said earnestly at her interview. *'I could tell you everything about that pendant there! It'd been worn by Princess Yulia. During the war of—'*

Patrick had cut her off. *'I can't wait to hear more!*

Such passion! It will no doubt serve you well behind my counter, ringing up orders.'

She'd been so nervous she had not even noted the sarcasm. It didn't matter anyway. She'd no choice after her parents cut her off but to take the only job she could get—well, the only job she was willing to do.

'You should sell feet pics online!' a friend had suggested.

'You should absolutely get fucked,' Serena had retorted.

Serena squinted, glanced back at the hallway, and turned the volume up a single digit.

Heheh, she cackled internally. *I win.*

Then she rested on her elbow, huffed, and looked around the store. Any moment now, she was going to be asked to dust again. Antique shops were *supposed* to be a little dusty, it preserved the history as it was found. But no, once an hour on the dot, another dusting.

She checked the time. It'd been five minutes since she should have done it, and yet the call never came. She pricked her pointy ears towards the backroom, wondering what he was getting up to. No doubt searching the internet for new tombs, or however it was they found them.

Serena got up, swung her legs around the counter in a move that would've made her feel badass had she not slipped and nearly fallen flat on her face.

"Ow!" she cried. Her ankle stung mercilessly.

That's what she got for not wearing her boots. She was just glad she didn't have to wear them when she was alone. Some men got funny about feet. Apparently, there was a whole industry behind it.

"What's happening back there?" Michael called.

"Nothing!" she cried, then strolled over to the books, tracing her finger across them. She picked up one she'd been meaning to read again. *The Legend of Juniper the Bard: From Humble Beginnings to Fame across the Realms.*

The cover depicted a short, white-haired elven bard. She was an adorable potato.

For some reason, Serena felt an affinity with this strange high elf from the past. Juniper was said to be different. She'd not fitted in, either.

CHAPTER

THREE

MICHAEL

Well, that was...unusual, Michael thought, leaning back in his uncle's comfortable chair. The rich mahogany gleamed from age and varnish, and the leather cushions stitched into it were squishy.

Patrick's desk was made of a similar wood, and was way oversized, like something belonging to a mob boss.

"Nice, though," Michael muttered, tapping his finger against the grain.

Two chairs sat upon the other side of the room, a table between them. Michael wondered if Patrick ever entertained in here.

He arched his neck to spot the map of the realms tacked up on the wall, with pins upon the places he'd visited. *Good thing he visited the top two corners of the map first,* Michael thought with a snicker. He was sure he'd heard that joke from somewhere, but if nobody else knew where, he was happy to pretend he'd come up with it, when he said it again in company.

He tapped his fingers against his stomach, giving a little huff. "What does that guy do all day?"

Michael supposed that Patrick had plenty of explorers and tomb raiders on the job, so he just had to sit and wait to receive them. He twitched his nose. It would be easier if that drow wasn't out there, and then he could busy himself with busywork.

Well, he could still do that? Maybe just accept it'd be under her watchful eye. Those crimson eyes sort of creeped him out. They'd stared into his soul and plucked out all the porn he'd watched on the family computer as a youth.

He got up, strolled through the hallway, and entered the doorframe. Serena was tapping away at her phone, the long black nails on her fingers not obscuring her ability to type at record pace—no doubt complaining to a girlfriend about her horrible new boss.

Some beads hung on the side of the doorframe, pulled along the edge by a hook. Michael frowned and pulled them back, revealing a curtain that mostly obscured the hallway from the rest of the store.

"Wonder why that was hooked up," Michael said.

"Patrick wants to keep an eye on the shop," Serena replied.

"No need for that when you're here." Michael stretched and yawned. "I'm heading to the store. Want anything?"

"No thanks," she said bluntly, glancing at him.

Michael resisted a chuckle. *Difficult*. That was what she was.

"All right then," he said. "You got any diet restrictions? You know, for the future?"

"Nope," she said, frowning at him and brushing a curtain of black-and-white hair out of her face.

A white stripe went along the back of her messy, tied-back bun. He had to admit it looked pretty cool. Shame it was on such a *difficult* person. Yeah, that was the polite way to describe her. Maybe he'd have some less polite ways when he had supper with his brother later.

Still, he knew the way to any difficult person's heart was through their stomach.

Maybe she was just hungry.

∼

Michael returned through the door with a *ding*. Some customers were browsing the books section, and Serena tapped away on her phone, her glasses reflecting her screen.

He squinted, trying to spot what she was looking at. She scowled at him, and he quickly looked away.

"Afternoon," he said to a pretty, slender catkin

who licked her fingers as she turned the page of the book she was browsing. She had messy blonde hair, fluffy blonde ears, and a thin, golden tail swishing back and forth from the hole cut in her *very* tight jeans.

He'd had a few one-night stands with catkins. They were great in the sack, and terrifying out of it.

She glanced up at him, then gave him a second look with more of a smile.

"Hi there," she purred.

"Let me know if there's anything I can help with," Michael replied.

The catkin snapped the book shut.

In the periphery of Michael's eye, he saw Serena had looked up from her riveting social media browsing.

"Yes!" The catkin bounced on the toes of her sneakers. They were the kind grill-dads wore that were inexplicably in fashion for kids now. However, he judged this woman as about nineteen or twenty. "I was wondering if you knew anything about the ancient history of my kind?" she asked. "I'm writing an essay at university, and everything on the internet is so untrustworthy these days!"

"Well," Michael began, "I know a little about your history. In fact, I've seen a few monuments to Lady Rathe in my time."

The catkin gasped, and her slitted pupils swelled as she gazed upon Michael with a heightened fascination.

Suddenly, stomping boots sauntered past them. The catkin's eyes followed behind Michael, and then the bell at the door rang.

"We're closing for lunch, everybody!" Serena said, as if she was calling last orders at the pub.

"Another time," Michael said.

"Sure, another time." The catkin grinned her sparkling, pointy teeth.

The customers left the store, and Serena shunted the key in the lock with far more force than was necessary, turning it with a hefty clunk. She flipped the sign on the board.

"I'm not sure the boss would appreciate you kicking out our customers before they buy something," Michael said. "I was just about to make a sale."

"I wanted to express my appreciation for the lunch you got me," Serena replied, "by being able to eat it in peace, even though I asked you not to. Thanks." It was the most sullen, monotone 'thanks' Michael had ever heard.

"How'd you know I got you anything?" he asked. "This might all be for me. I'm a growing lad."

"You asked me if I had any dietary restrictions. Unless you were calling me fat, I'm not sure why you'd care." She crossed her arms under her *definitely-appropriate-to-be-called* fat breasts.

"Fair enough." Michael dug into his bag and pulled out a wrapped-up bagel.

Serena's eyes lit up. She swallowed. "Thanks," she

said as Michael handed over the bagel. She walked over to the counter, putting that wall of protection between them again.

There was a chair and a desk beside the corner of the wall, and Michael nabbed the chair, put it on the other side of the counter, and pulled out his bagel—pulled pork and mustard.

Meanwhile, Serena took a great bite of her salmon and cream cheese, her eyes glazed over in bliss. He couldn't quite say exactly why he thought that selection would be best for her. He recalled reading a book once about a chesty goth cashier who loved them, so he felt it appropriate to get that for Serena, considering how much Serena reminded him of that moody mage.

She nibbled on the bagel, smiling to herself with her pretty, full black lips, and Michael was pleased to see he was right.

Even though he didn't cook it, there was something satisfying about watching someone enjoy a meal you'd provided.

Even someone like her.

He considered how nice his uncle was in giving her a job. It wasn't easy, finding one as a drow in the human realm, and as far as he'd seen, she wasn't the slightest bit grateful for it, or even trying to be easy to work with.

He took another bite. The air became stifled by the awkwardness of their silence.

"What brings you here, anyway?" Michael asked.

"*Here*?" Serena replied with a dubious squint. She had a bit of cream cheese on her thumb and lifted it to her mouth. She pushed out her lips as she suckled on the cream, maintaining eye contact with him as her cheeks hollowed from the sensual motion.

"The store, or Stonereach. You choose." Michael frowned at her, wondering just what her game was.

"I studied here," she said. "Silly name, considering it's all metal and glass skyscrapers."

"Things are named before they become other things. So, fresh out of education, then?" he asked, trying to deduce her age. She could've been nineteen, she could have been nine hundred. It was hard to tell with these elven types, let alone half-elves.

"Flunked," she said.

"Sorry to hear that."

"And my mother said that if I didn't at least succeed in the terrible degree I'd chosen, then I'd have to—" She paused, licked her thumb again, and scowled at Michael. "What's it to you, anyway?"

"Just making conversation," Michael said.

"Fair," she said, no doubt holding back some choice words. Michael suspected she was mad at him for being invasive. "I'm..." she began, then paused and reached over to the radio to put it on. Rock music—some band from the nineties—played at an acceptable volume.

Michael looked around the store. Dim orange

lights cast a calming glow upon all the artifacts, and a light coat of dust was beginning to coat everything.

"This place needs a dust," he said.

"Fine," she said, grunting under her breath. She put the bagel down, brushed her hands, and made to get up.

"Sit down, enjoy your lunch!" Michael said. "I'll do it. Gods know I've got no idea what my uncle does all day, anyway. I've never been much involved in that side of the business. My fixers sort out the jobs for me."

Her lips tightened. "Thanks for lunch," she said. "Are you in tomorrow? I'll get you something then. What would you like?"

"Surprise me," Michael said, finishing his bagel and brushing his hands off. He was confident he was getting a little bit of a read on the woman. She wasn't rude to him, specifically, she was just rude to her very core. That made him feel a little more understanding.

People were never like that unless they'd had some awful reason to be. He suspected something had to do with her parents, or simply the hardships of being a drow.

Michael tried not to grin, because he'd decided he wouldn't rise to her bait. He would kill her with kindness.

∼

"You have no idea what you're talking about!" Michael yelled, dust rag in hand as he leaned on the potion rack. "It's perfectly acceptable. Just because the court's got strict laws about it doesn't mean it's not okay! What the hells would you know, sitting here on your butt?"

The day had gone by as well as it could've, with them making idle chat and keeping out of each other's way. Several hours later, and close to closing time, the topic came up of Michael's vocation.

"It's completely unconscionable!" Serena yelled back. "Sacred places of people's history, desecrated so you can make a few coin." She held her hand up with fingers spread wide in frustration, as if this would make her point more correct.

A bunch of customers had looked up from their browsing and were now watching with wild enjoyment, and some looked a little horrified.

"What's the difference between me and some adventurer seeking chests of gold and weaponry in dungeons?" Michael asked, taking a deep breath to calm himself.

"Because those are *dungeons*!"

"Tombs are just dungeons with a more famous rich person in them!" he yelled, returning to her level again. "Those enchanted skeletons don't appear out of thin air, you know."

"Obviously, you know nothing about magic, because some *very* much do."

Michael resisted a laugh. *Okay*, he thought. *That was a good retort.*

"It's not funny," she snarled, crossing her arms, which made her hefty, swollen bosom fatten even more. A blue vein danced along the sensual curve.

"Ahem," a customer said, scratching the back of his neck. "Can I just..."

"What!" Serena snapped at him.

Suddenly, the force of her glowering relinquished from Michael. He felt a thousand times lighter and realized they had just been yelling at each other amongst the customers—and this was after kicking them out earlier to eat their lunch.

He was doing an exceptionally poor job of looking after his uncle's store and suspected now that the entire point of his being asked to do it was to keep Patrick's employee in check. *Yeah, doing a great job at that*, he thought.

Michael decided to set some boundaries, assert some authority, and, most of all, not tell her the excellent retort he'd just thought of.

He aggressively ran the duster over the potions, making them so shining clean that he could see his face in them.

The retort was this: if she had such a problem with his vocation, then why the hells was she working in a store that depended on it?

Yeah, he wouldn't say that. He'd rant about it later with his brother.

CHAPTER
FOUR

SERENA

"He's an asshole!" she said, stirring her mai tai.

The cocktail bar played awful tropical music. Why did Calra always insist they come here? Neither of them was acclimated to the sun. Drow liked the depths. Orcs liked the mountains. Even back home in the outside realm of Ilgath, her people tended to stay indoors.

Calra brushed a brown, braided lock of hair behind her serrated ear. "Crush his skull," she grunted. "Drink the juice from his brains."

"You can't just crush a person's skull every time they look at you funny," Serena said, scowling at her pretty orc friend.

Her tusks gleamed with rings, and her large orange

eyes considered Serena with pity and then a light smirk.

"You're fucking with me," Serena said.

The bartender chuckled, and Serena snapped her gaze at him. He held his hands up and went to bother someone else.

"Serena, babe," Calra said. "Everywhere you go, everyone is an asshole. I say this because I love you. Maybe *you*'re the asshole?"

"It's possible for everyone to be an asshole and me to be one too!" Serena huffed, knowing Calra was likely right. "Another drink, please," she called to the bartender and stared him deeply in the eyes.

He walked over with a smile, and when her unwavering gaze would not break from his, he glanced away uncomfortably.

"I'm going to say this very slowly," Serena said, "so that you don't ask '*What, are you sure?*'"

He frowned, nodding.

"Vodka," she said. "Straight," she added, then leaned forward. "Pint," she finished. "Got it?"

"Isn't that a little—" he began.

She closed her eyes and gave a deep sigh that suggested she was about to *crush his skull and drink the juice from his brains*.

"Got it!" the bartender said.

Calra mouthed 'sorry' at the bartender.

Serena huffed. "You may have a point."

"Sure, I have a point. He didn't deserve that."

"But he was going to question it, and *hmm* and *hah*, as if he'd never even served a drow before!"

"Elves don't drink much, so he probably hasn't, let alone a drow."

"Well, that means I need more to feel something because of our affinity against poisons!"

"A pint of vodka will make you feel more than *something*, or maybe you'll just pass out and feel nothing at all."

"One can hope," Serena said, holding up her mai tai without looking at Calra. The orc clinked it, and they gulped their silly cocktails in one gulp.

Then, the bartender arrived with the clear, water-looking drink, and an expression half of annoyance, half of intrigue.

"I am sorry," Serena said to him. "I've had a very stressful day, which isn't fair on you."

"Most people here have had stressful days," he said, smiling, a glint in his teeth. "If there's any way I could help make it better..." He leaned a bit more forward, the hint in his words as clear as day.

Serena's lips tightened. She leaned closer and licked her lips, making her eyes go sultry. "Some salty crisps would be great!" she said, with a bright, cheery tone like a children's TV presenter. "And maybe the link to your review page, so I can complain about the creepy bartender who didn't want the giant tip I was about to give him."

He cleared his throat. "Coming right up."

Calra snorted. "You cruel bitch." Then she called the bartender. "Bucket of beer, please."

"You'd be a cruel bitch too if you were me," Serena mumbled, taking off her glasses and rubbing them with her top. "It's fine. I'll tip him more anyway to make up for it."

"That doesn't make up for it," Calra said, then she brightened up and nudged her shoulder. "Hey, you know what you need?"

Serena winced, looking at the dance floor behind her. It was mostly empty except for some drunk-looking crackwhores and a mustached man holding a briefcase, who nodded to the music, completely off-beat. Why did Calra always insist on coming to this stupid place and *dancing*? It was likely because the clientele here was just as weird as they were, or maybe because Calra worked as a bouncer here on weekends, so she got a discount on her drinks.

Serena sighed, rubbing her fishnet-covered arm. It felt less fashionably-gothic here, like she had stolen one of the actual fish nets hanging on the wall as decoration.

"Go on then, what do I need?" Serena asked, anticipating being forced to dance like Calra always made her.

"A great, big, thunderous orgasm."

The bartender choked, put the bucket of beer down, and swiftly left the vicinity, perhaps to reconsider his life and return to college to get that degree.

"You need a good, hard, dicking down, I think. Get that cuntyness railed right out of you."

Serena closed her eyes. "Maybe go back to the orgasm. That only horrified me a little."

∼

Arm in arm, Serena and Calra swayed across the street.

"*Working eight to—*" Serena belched. "*Ten. Ain't no way to make a living.*"

"Th-th-th-" Calra stammered. "That's not the lyrics, you dumb bitch."

"Don't call me a dumb bitch, you stinking brute."

"I don't stink!" Calra sniffled a tear. She was always very sensitive about her smell because orcs tended to be quite pungent if they didn't take care of it. She showered three times a day.

"You..." Serena grabbed her friend's muscled arm and lifted it, then smushed her nose into her armpit and gave it a whiff. "You smell quite nice, actually."

"I know!" Calra pushed her off and held her arms.

Serena looked at the moon. The silver orb was blurry, and she shaded her forehead with her hand for some reason, as if that would make it clearer.

Moon goddess, Serena thought. *Won't ye guide me the way?*

"It's this way, ya dumb bitch."

"I didn't say anything!" Serena snapped at Calra.

"You were talking all fancy like. *Ye* and *thus*. Like it was the ol-ol—*hiccup*—old times."

Huh, Serena thought. *I could have sworn I was thinking that. Okay, what am I thinking...now! Purple monkey dishwasher.* She put her hands on her hips and stared at the orc.

Calra scowled. "Why are you looking at me like that? Was it about what we talked about earlier? Stay back, thesbian!"

"I'm not a thesbian! Fuck off!" Serena snapped.

"You are! Saying words like *ye* and *thus*."

"And it isn't spelled like lesbian. It's thes-*pi*-an, not thes-*bi*-an."

"Alright, Herwhione. You would know. You're the theh-theh—" Calra sneezed violently. "—thesbian."

"Thespian!"

"Oi!" came a voice from above. The girls looked up to see a middle-aged woman with a towel wrapped around her hair, hanging out the window above the kebab shop. "It's one a.m. on a Tuesday. Shut up!"

But a delicious, meaty scent had drifted up Serena's nostrils. She sniffed, and so did Calra. Their gazes fell to the kebab shop. It glowed a glorious aura, like a finally discovered treasure.

And angels sang a heavenly song.

That might've just been the hum from the rotisserie machine.

Soon enough, they left the kebab shop, digging into their delicious, greasy, meaty meals, stumbling over on their way back to Serena's apartment.

"Mmmmm," they hummed in unison, clumsily eating the meat and salad in a pita bread. "So good," Serena said.

"I hope whoever invented kebab is getting his dick sucked," Calra said.

"You are so godsdamn foul," Serena said. "And anyway, he was from the far east, so he's probably got a harem lining up on a conveyor belt to suck him off until the sun rises."

"Good lad," Calra said. "Oi, I was wondering—" She expressed with her fork, which bashed Serena's arm, and Serena stumbled a little. A bit of salad dropped onto the floor.

Serena grinned at Calra and said, "That was close! Can you imagine if I dropped it?"

She turned back to walk in the way, and her right Dick Marvin caught on the loose shoelace of her left Dick Marvin, and she crashed down into the ground, smashing her knee into the concrete, then her chin. Her glasses flew off into the distance.

"Fuck!"

"No, babe, it's alright!" Calra said.

Serena rolled onto her back, looking up at the nostrils of her orc friend.

"It's not alright!" Serena's lower lip trembled, making her chin hurt even more.

She sat up, arched her neck, and turned to see the blurry brown shape behind her. A little further in the distance were some smaller blurry green and brown shapes—her precious kebab, lost to the pavement.

"It's alright," Calra said, grabbing Serena by the arm and lifting her. "You can share mine."

∽

The two girls sat on Serena's couch, watched by framed posters of rock bands and one of a beautiful, haunted landscape. Some people thought it was a piece of art painted by some dead guy, but others knew it as a poster of *The Lands Betwix*—the main setting of her favorite video game, *Elven Ring*.

The TV was off—a black mirror of doom, reflecting the two girls pigging out on the kebab they shared between their laps, on top of the covers.

"I love ya, babe," Calra said, stifling another belch. Her eyes were glazed over with tiredness, and she pushed over the kebab box to Serena.

"You can't be serious," Serena said. "You've hardly eaten it."

Calra put her head down on the side of the couch, so Serena finished up the meal, staring in adoration at the orc.

Calra opened her eyes. "Why ya looking at me like that for?"

"I was just w-w-wondering," Serena said, stifling a

yawn as she sat down on the other side of the couch. "Do you like yourself?"

"Of course I do! I've got muscles for days, I can bench a...bench a—" She yawned "—a very large amount, and I've got glutes as strong as mithril. What's not to like?"

"Nothing," Serena said, sighing as she pulled the covers, stealing them a little from the orc.

"Why'd you ask?" Calra asked through another yawn.

Serena stared at herself in the black mirror of the television. "I don't like myself very much," she said softly.

Calra replied with a snore.

∼

MICHAEL

"By the gods, what happened to you?" Michael exclaimed, eyebrows raised in surprise.

In the dining room of his brother's apartment, he stared in disbelief at the bold shiner on Tommy's eye. The kid had strolled in about twenty minutes late for supper with a wide grin—as if proud of his new injury.

Michael immediately looked at his brother for an explanation as his sister-in-law, Orla, fussed over her son.

"He's still got to have a job," Wilson explained,

digging his fork into his tuna steak and tearing off a piece. His well-groomed face had a sly smile. Was he proud of Tommy for this? *Like father like son*, Michael supposed.

Michael shook his head. This was why he never had kids. Well, one of the reasons.

As gentle jazz music played on the radio in the miniature suburbia of an apartment, Michael decided the best words to choose.

Wilson chose them for him. "He's following in your footsteps," he said.

"Could he follow in footsteps that don't disappear beneath your feet?" Michael replied, staring at his brother.

They could have been twins if Michael had chosen the office life, combed his hair, moisturized daily, and slept regularly in a bed. The list went on of what Michael could've done instead of tomb raiding.

Maybe he should've, because apparently you couldn't stop kids doing what they wanted. He thought parents were supposed to have control over their kid's life.

"He's eighteen," Wilson explained quietly. "I'd rather he tells me about these things than does it anyway and hides it. At least then I can offer some guidance."

"Whatever happened to 'my house my rules'?" *And what guidance?* Michael wondered. *You never took up our father's mantle. I did.*

"Well, somebody's got to do it," Wilson said as Orla took her son to the bathroom to clean him up.

Michael scowled. "He's not my responsibility. I thought I was doing him a favor, maybe saving his life."

"By putting him in the hands of someone else?"

"Stop him doing it then. You're his father!" Michael rubbed his eyes. "You can't tell me Orla approves of this. No, enough of this. I'm getting crap from work, and now I'm giving crap at dinner. Let's just forget it."

"I thought you, of all people, would understand our lineage. Just because I rejected it to be with Orla doesn't mean my son can." Wilson put down his fork and grunted.

"I said drop it," Michael grunted harder.

There was a silence, and the two men seethed with unsaid words.

Michael thought that Wilson was living vicariously through his son, encouraging him to do what he no longer could.

"Pint?" Wilson asked.

"Pint," Michael confirmed.

His brother got up and walked over to the kitchen, where the hiss of a bottle opening made Michael anticipate the taste of the beverage already.

He brought the drink in, and they drank in a little more comfortable silence.

"Got a party tomorrow," Wilson said.

"You? A party?" Michael said in disbelief.

"It's a work thing," Wilson said sheepishly.

"Oh, well, that's a shame. It means I can't go."

"Guests are *welcome*." Wilson grinned. "Besides, it will be good for you. Get you out of the house. Maybe you'll meet someone."

"Not sure you want me damaging your reputation." Michael grinned.

"Damage it? You're my badass brother. You'll up my cool points by over nine thousand with the kids, *dude*."

"Nobody talks like that anymore. No wonder the interns think you're lame."

"Hey, I never told you that!"

They laughed, cleared up their plates, and retired to the couch, where Wilson used his phone to transport the jazz music there electronically from the dining room. Michael would not bring up that you were supposed to listen to this music on vinyl, only because then he'd be forced to admit that, yes, it was much more convenient not to have to get up every so often to turn the record, blow on the record, or place the record back in a sleeve to grab another.

It wasn't like he could carry records around with him anyway, but dammit, they were better, and he'd fight that cause to the end.

He looked at the picture of his father and uncle beside the two kids in their expedition gear. Their mother had long died since that photo. Michael could barely remember her.

"Patrick ever mention his employee?" Michael asked.

"That drow bitch?" Wilson replied.

Michael raised his eyebrows. He'd never heard his brother speak like that. "You've met her, then?" he asked.

"No, I'm just quoting Patrick," he said, absent-mindedly flicking through the channels of the muted television.

Michael frowned. "Suppose I shouldn't be surprised that he doesn't like her. I wonder why he keeps her around, then."

"She must be good at her job."

"Doubt that, judging from what I saw today."

"Maybe he's...you know." Wilson gave Michael a seedy grin.

Michael snarled. "Doubt *that* even more." He took a larger swig of beer, relaxing on the way-too-comfortable couch. He felt like he would sink into it and never return. He'd been having trouble sleeping on it when it was pulled out as a bed.

"Did you go to visit him?" Michael asked.

Wilson nodded. "He looks very, very still."

That was the last they spoke of it, but Michael urged himself to visit him when he could, not that it would matter. Patrick was in stasis.

They continued drinking, watching an action

movie on TV as Orla joined them with wine. At some point, Michael thought he'd get Orla on her own to see if he could convince *her* to knock some sense into her son. Then he shook his head.

It wasn't his place. It wasn't his business.

CHAPTER
FIVE

MICHAEL

"Round two," Michael mumbled to himself, opening the door to *Relics of Wonder*. Except the door didn't budge, and the sign was still flipped to closed. He checked his watch. It was half nine, a beautiful day with the sun shining, and Serena hadn't shown up for work.

"To be expected," he said, digging through his pocket and finding his spare key for the shop among the several thousand others he had in there.

Upon entering, he flicked on the light, and the vintage lampshade filled the room with a dim orange glow. The place was already filthy with dust. How in the hells did it attract it so easily?

Michael strolled through the goods, walked to the counter, looked at the cash machine, and blinked.

It wasn't the old style he used as a kid. This one had a touch screen he had no idea how to use. He mashed a finger against the screen. It asked him to log in.

Tightening his lips, Michael rushed to the back room—getting tangled in the beads and feeling like he was trapped in vines in a tomb—and walked over to the office, looking over the folders on one of the shelves. He then saw the diary on the desk, which he ran over to and found a bunch of phone numbers.

It's Michael. What's the login details to the cash register? he texted Serena, then tapped his phone against the desk mat, waiting for a response.

Finally, his phone vibrated.

Be there soon, Serena replied.

"I didn't ask you that, did I?" Michael grumbled.

When? Michael texted as he stood up and made his way to the counter. He supposed he could just take cash from the customers if any arrived, though he wouldn't be able to give them change. He frowned. **Can I just get the login details?** he double texted. Tommy had once told him that double texting was a heinous crime. Tommy could fuck off, and so could Serena.

Serena replied quickly. **Username: Admin. Password: Wendy.**

Suddenly, Michael bloomed with a wash of emotion as memories came flooding back. Wendy was his childhood dog, and Patrick used to look after her all the time. He felt a fondness then for his uncle and even greater shame in not visiting him. But Patrick *had* said to just come and look after the shop. He was probably too proud to be seen in the condition he was in.

Doesn't mean I shouldn't go, Michael thought.

Soon enough, the door opened with a whine, the bell dinged, and Serena walked in wearing black sunglasses.

She walked with a fragile slowness, as if she might fall apart at any moment. The baggy black hoodie around her chest only solidified the image.

Michael crossed his arms and gazed at her. Her fishnet tights had a huge rip in them, and she wore the same denim skirt as yesterday. Her lovely, thick thighs jiggled a little as her heavy boots stomped the floor despite her careful movements.

"Are you feeling unwell?" Michael asked, resisting a smirk at knowing exactly what she was feeling.

"A little under the weather," she crooned, like an old lady. Then she cleared her throat, closing a fist against her chest. "Ahem," she said, much more youthfully. And then she gulped, probably trying not to be sick.

Michael tried not to smirk even harder, knowing she could be looking at him behind those sunglasses.

"You should've called in sick," he said, thinking he wouldn't have minded.

"Need to be paid," she replied.

He frowned. "You don't get sick pay?"

"Why would I get sick pay?" she snapped, walking over to the counter and standing before him. Michael was in her seat.

"Go to the backroom," he said.

"Excuse me?" A snarl of confusion formed on her pretty black lips.

"Go sleep," he said. "I'll stay on the shop floor today."

Serena looked at the hallway, and her snarl turned to one of disgust. "It's okay. I can work. Let me just make some coffee first."

Michael frowned. What sort of retail employee wouldn't jump at the chance to sleep in the back office and not have to talk to customers?

"Are you sure?" he asked, looking at the counter. He really could not handle another day in the office, bored out of his mind.

Serena looked again at the hallway, cocking her head in perhaps consideration. "Can I order some food?" she asked.

"Certainly." Michael's stomach rumbled.

"I'm gonna order some food and coffee. Do you want anything?"

Michael looked at the front display, where the light was barely creeping in. It was a beautiful day today, not that that mattered, being trapped in the shop.

Serena was hungover, and Michael didn't feel like seeing how moody she could get in front of customers when she was like this.

He could torture her, of course, by making her work and giving her lots of tasks as revenge for how she'd spoken to him yesterday. But that would not be killing her with kindness. Better yet, he was about to be the best boss ever. *Oh, gods,* he thought, *this is how my brother thinks.*

"I'll make you a deal," Michael said.

Serena crossed her arms.

But Michael walked over and locked the door, flipping the sign from open to closed.

"Patrick will throw a fit," Serena said, looking over her sunglasses at him.

Some eyes undressed people. Serena's eyes deskinned them.

"Patrick's in stasis," Michael said, shuddering at her crimson orbs. "I'm in charge now, and I say we're gonna take a day off."

"And do what?"

"Well, you're gonna order us a pizza."

Serena gulped, fighting something back down to her stomach.

"Maybe a nice simple bacon sandwich?" Michael suggested instead.

She nodded.

∽

They sat cross-legged on the floor of the shop, between two of the shelves.

"Good night, last night then?" Michael asked.

Serena shrugged, then frowned. "What do you mean? I wasn't doing anything."

"You must think I'm dumb."

She sighed, then pulled her sunglasses off. The lines underneath her red eyes were frightening. Then she hid them a little with her regular glasses.

"Must've been a good night," Michael concluded.

"I—" she began, and then her phone vibrated, and the food arrived. She rushed over, stepping over Michael, giving him a lovely view of her light-purple thighs, up her shirt, and a whiff of her perfume and some gentle woman's sweat. Drow smelled nice—sort of, sweet.

Eventually, she returned, bringing with her the tantalizing smell of bacon and two coffees steaming away.

She dropped down again, pulling her skirt down, not before revealing a further view of the underside of her thigh and the black frilly fabric protecting her modesty between her legs. A faint curve of her buttocks was revealed before she obscured it with her skirt.

She dug into the bag and handed him the sandwich wrapped in foil and then something else.

"What's this?" Michael asked, picking up the packet of crisps.

"Obviously, you've never seen a gun," Serena said sardonically.

It was a packet of ham and mustard crisps, the sandwich filling he'd eaten before. He hadn't even told her what one it was he'd gotten, but she'd noticed.

"Thanks," he said, frowning, a little confused.

"Real weird taste in sandwiches," she said. "Surprised they even made that in crisps."

"Was my dad's favorite," Michael replied.

She blinked at him. "Sorry," she said.

"No, it's fine. It's my favorite, too."

"So you just, like, love to bring up awkward stuff to one-up me?"

"I don't do that!"

"Not anymore, you don't." She grinned at him.

Michael just scowled at that. Was that her attempt at ribbing him?

They ate away while Serena seemed to struggle to breathe from her hangover. Her skin was varnished with sweat. She pulled her hoody up and over herself, revealing the same crop-top corset she'd worn yesterday—black with frilly lace edges, pushing up violently on her giant tits. Like her face, her tits glistened with sweat. The blue lightning vein was even more apparent as it zigzagged down the tantalizing curve.

Michael swallowed. A dark purple areola horizoned from the cleavage, just a small part, but very obvious.

He continued to eat his sandwich while, in the

corner of his eye, she fixed herself, seeming not to have noticed his watching.

The air was stifled with a thick silence.

"So, do you like—" Serena began, swallowing. "—play games?"

"Erm, like videogames?"

"Sure," she said.

"Not for years," Michael said. "Too busy with work."

She scoffed. "The *one* guy who doesn't."

"Well, I'm a little older than you," he said.

"Wanna bet?" she replied.

"In looks, at least. You don't look a day over eighteen."

Serena twitched her cute nose at him. "Take a guess," she said.

"How the hells should I know?" Michael sipped his coffee.

"You're the expert in other cultures."

"I'm more of an appreciator from afar."

"Not from far enough."

"Oh, here we go again." Michael rolled his eyes, taking a bite of a sandwich.

Serena leaned back, grunting as she tore off her boots and put her legs out. Her bare feet, toes poking through the fishnets, were right by his thigh, and his eye line traveled up her legs, and the merciless way they fattened from her sitting down.

He swallowed.

"Take a guess," Serena said. "I won't be offended. That's a human thing."

Michael shrugged. "Four hundred."

She covered her mouth and giggled. Michael did not think he'd ever heard her laugh before. It was sort of musical.

"What?" he asked.

"I'm a half-elf," she replied.

"What does that mean, exactly?"

"It means I don't possess anything near a pure elven length of life."

"So... four hundred isn't a good guess, then?"

"Try thirty," she said.

"Oh." He looked at her, struggling to see her as thirty. It seemed that she was really just a nineteen-year-old, especially physically. She was totally in the prime of her life.

"I'll live hundreds of years," she said. "Not thousands."

"Still, that's a lot."

"To you, maybe." She took another sip of coffee, then brushed her skirt free of crumbs. "How do you feel about drow?" she asked.

"How do I feel about them?" Michael repeated, shrugging. "I think they're rude—" Her jaw dropped. "—needlessly antagonistic—" Her eyes widened. "—irresponsible with others' time—" She smirked when she realized he was just talking about her. "—and a hot mess," he concluded, grinning at her.

"Wait, you think I'm hot?" she gasped, fluttering her chest, making her bosom jiggle mercilessly from the impact.

"I was talking about drow in general," Michael replied, his face turning hot. "And I didn't say hot. I said a hot mess."

"Exactly. You didn't say mess. You said a *hot* mess."

Change tactic, Michael thought. *Quickly, before she wins.*

"Did it work?" he asked, absentmindedly taking a sip of his coffee.

"Did *what* work?" she asked.

"Was that all it took to get you not to dislike me?"

Serena scowled at Michael, then bunched her sandwich wrapping into a ball and threw it at him. She then got up. "We should probably open the shop," she said, looking away from him.

Loud and clear, Michael thought.

∽

SERENA

Serena crossed her arms, daring him to look at them again. But Michael just stared at *her* like she was stupid.

"I've seen them!" he said. "They were real!"

They certainly are, Serena thought. *I dare you to look at them again.*

Serena shrugged. "Could just be made up. Lots of things are made up."

"But I dug out the damn sword myself! Saw the stinking ruby on the hilt."

"Could be fake. You looked inside their coffins?" Serena raised her eyebrows. "Wow. *That's* a new low. Besides, they could be *anyone's* skeletons. Did she have a tail?"

"Well, I didn't see that." Michael shook his head in disbelief.

"Then it wasn't her. Tails don't have bones."

"Tails *do* have bones. Are you insane? I meant I didn't see the skeleton, not her tailbone."

Serena resisted a grin. This was fun.

"You're fucking with me," Michael said, his shoulders relaxing.

"Got to pass the time somehow," she replied, biting her tongue.

"I can't wait for this week to be over," Michael said with a yawn.

"Then what, you gonna go back to your sacrilege?"

"Yes, actually. What will you do?"

"Go back to your cunty uncle."

Michael blinked at her, he looked at the door, then walked over through the shelves, and she heard the distinct *thunk* of the door locking.

"What are you doing? I'll scream." Serena said, half joking, half nervous.

"Oh, shut up," Michael said, appearing from the

hallways. "Right," he said. "Something's up. So I wanna know what it is right now."

"What do you mean?"

She avoided his gaze, as he stared daggers into her.

"With you and my uncle," Michael said.

"Eww, are you serious!" Serena feigned misunderstanding.

"No, I didn't...why does everyone think I mean that? No, listen." Michael walked a bit closer.

Serena stood a bit straighter, leaning away from him. "What?" she asked, looking away.

"Do you and my uncle not get along?" he asked.

"He doesn't get along with me," she replied.

"Well..." Michael looked like he was holding some words in. She did not have to imagine hard what they were. "I'm not him," he finally said.

"But you're related, you'll tell him what I say. Or your brother you're staying with, and then he'll tell him, and Patrick will just make my life an even deeper layer of hell."

"Why don't you quit?" Michael asked.

"And do what, sell feet pics?"

"You've got the feet for it."

"Ugh, what the fuck!"

"It was a joke." Michael batted away the air nonchalantly.

"No, it wasn't. I've got lovely feet." She turned up her nose, not daring to look at him.

Then, they both burst into laughter.

"He's really not kind to you, then?" Michael asked. "And not just because you're a moody bitch?"

"I wasn't so moody when I started," she said. "But please don't say anything. I need to pay my rent."

"Alright. I won't say anything," he said.

"Promise?"

Michael held out his hand, and they shook.

"Friends?" Michael asked.

"Don't push it." Serena let go and looked away, though, a flicker of a smile appeared on the side of her mouth. "Acquaintances," she said, then forced a frown so that her smile would go away.

"Isn't that a step behind coworkers?" he asked.

"You are *so* annoying." Her smile turned into a frown for real, and she turned up the radio to her favorite rock station.

CHAPTER SIX

MICHAEL

Michael adjusted his shirt, rolling up the sleeves to the forearm because Orla had told him girls liked that. She'd said this after knocking on the door to offer him a cup of tea.

Orla's such a gem, Michael thought. *Wilson's lucky to have her.*

As Michael stared at himself, wondering if he should go for one top button undone or two, he found himself happy for his brother. Back in the day, he'd been appalled that Wilson would reject their heritage. Even further back in the day, such a thing was unconscionable. If you were born a Seeker, you were an adventuring relic hunter, and that was that. His last name had even been chosen to express that. Michael Seeker doubted it was an accident he was named that.

Though that wasn't even his name. Someone long ago had changed it to Walker.

It was a new age, a new time. And their father was dead. Michael just hoped he'd gotten over it, looking down on them from the heavens. After all, Wilson may have rejected their heritage, but without him, there would *be* no lineage to continue. It wasn't like Michael held any prospects for fatherhood. He couldn't stay in one place long enough to—

He shook his head. Tonight wasn't the time for such things. It was the time to have fun.

Michael looked over his cologne, the only one he ever had because a girl had complimented it once when he was younger, and now he was inseparable from the damn thing. *If it ain't broke, don't fix it.*

He left the bedroom, taking his pack and placing it back by the couch where he'd been sleeping, as his brother scrolled on his phone, his brogue shoes gleaming from a recent polish. Michael looked at his boots in the corner. He'd cleaned them, at least, but they wouldn't be gleaming. Ah well.

Wilson was already sipping on a beer.

"S'pose I'm driving then," Michael said.

"Nope. Getting a cab."

Damn, Michael thought. *I was going to use that as an excuse.* Michael enjoyed a beer now and again but was perfectly happy to be driving and then able to call it an early night.

Orla entered the room, wearing heels and a nice

summer dress. She passed Michael a beer. "You think we don't know your trick?" she said, laughing as she flicked her curly blonde lock out of her face. "You were pulling that all the time when we were kids. I swear, you're the only guy that *wants* to be the designated driver."

"You got me. I like an early night." Michael held up his hands. He then cracked open the beer and gave in to the occasion.

It wasn't quite early nights he liked, but recharging his batteries after being around people. Winner of the *Introvert of the Year* award, that was him.

"It's not gonna be some high school party with *spin the bottle* and *seven minutes in heaven*," Wilson said. "They're professionals."

"Pity," Orla said under her breath.

The two men both snapped their gazes at the blonde.

"And just what's *that* supposed to mean?" Michael said, giving her a look of incredulity.

"Nothing," she hummed, sipping on her beer.

"Oh my gods," Michael said. "Are you guys seeing this as some way for me to meet someone?"

"Why'd you think we're not letting you stay sober?" Wilson said.

"So you can watch me make a tit of myself?"

"And—" Wilson leaned forward and gave a shit-eating grin. "—the more you make a tit of yourself, showing off about all your grand adventures, the more likely you're going to meet someone."

"You said it's not a high school party, but this feels very high school, trying to set the dork up with a cheerleader."

They both snorted, and Wilson grabbed Michael's bicep. "Yeah right. You haven't been a dork in decades."

"I haven't got time for dating, anyway."

Though I do have time for a little fun, Michael thought, closing his eyes and submitting to it all.

As much as Michael tried to care about it, Wilson didn't seem to give a crap about the prospect of him spending a night with one of his co-workers.

∼

Marble countertops reflected lantern-like chandeliers —the kind that you could find in any old castle rusting away, or in a millionaire's home for several thousand dollars a pop.

The air smelled *clean.* Michael could practically see the maid staff slaving away for hours to get the place to look like this, day after day.

He held his champagne a little too tightly, sipping away at the bubbly liquid, craving a beer.

"And I said to him—" A tall, slender, pale elven woman stared deep into his eyes. "—if you don't want to meet the tail end of the viper, you best not try to fuck it in the arse."

Arse. Michael tried not to snicker.

The white-haired elf wore a pantsuit with deep cleavage. In a previous decade, she would've worn shoulder pads, no doubt. He could practically see them now, like pauldrons on a knight.

These were the real lords now, he told himself. Even if they never held the title.

"Ahem, Lady Elowen," a footman said. "The entrée's are ready to be served."

Oh crap, she actually is a noble! Michael racked his brain, trying to remember where she was from. *Elowen. Elowen...* He came up with nothing.

Lady Elowen picked one up delicately between her long nails, tasting the prawn and cream cheese thing.

"Delectable," she said, smacking her lips together like a pompous fish. *Apparently, you could taste food with your lips now.*

Michael was about to excuse himself when the elf touched his arm and said, "Excuse me, darling." Then she extended her hand to call out, "Bertrum, Bertrum! Did you get my email last night? I know! Hilarious, wasn't it!"

And Michael was alone at the party once more. He huffed, walked to the fridge, and helped himself to a tall boy. One thing was for sure, no matter how rich you got, you always liked a good beer.

High elves were funny creatures. They held the

keys to a past once kept a secret, but now they didn't see it as important. Decades flashed by in minutes for them. What did any of it matter? Obsession with the past was a human trait—a good thing, too, because otherwise, Michael wouldn't have a job.

This woman was probably thousands of years old. She might have even *met* the King's Knights. Michael bet he could get her to tell Serena they existed.

Michael snarled his nose. Nah. Serena knew they existed. She was just fucking with him.

"What you doing over here?" Wilson chided.

Michael's shoulder's untensed. He hadn't realized he was tensing them.

They clinked glasses. "Was just talking to Lady Elowen," Michael said.

Wilson's face fell.

"What?" Michael said in disbelief. "You said I'd be alright talking to anyone."

"Maybe anyone but the CEO!"

"We're at her house!"

Wilson just rubbed his face in distress.

"And we're eating her cheese." Michael dug into her fridge and grabbed a piece from the cheese board.

Wilson squinted, grinned, and grabbed a piece of cheese as well. "Anyway." He put his arm around Michael and brought him over to a group of his coworkers, where Wilson swiftly began showing off his exploits. The group seemed quite interested, asking Michael lots of questions and offering their expertise on a subject they had nil experience in. Michael got a lot of advice, which he took with a friendly smile while wishing a thousand curses upon them.

∼

SERENA

Serena snorted, sitting up in her bed. Her spaghetti string pajama top hung loose off her shoulder, a tit fallen out quite ungracefully. She fixed herself and smacked her lips. They were as dry as the desert.

"What time is it?" she murmured, grabbing her phone. It was only nine p.m. She'd thrown herself into bed the moment she'd gotten home from work—not before sluggishly getting out of her clothes because she absolutely could not sleep in the same clothes *two* nights in a row.

She stretched, sniffed at the sweat smell coming from her armpit, and scowled at the notification on her phone. It'd arrived an hour ago. From Michael.

"The fuck you want?" she said, feeling an odd feeling in her stomach—likely, her hangover still persisting.

Up to much tonight? the text read.

She tried not to smirk at how she'd left him waiting a very cool hour by accident. Now he would think she was cool, out doing very busy and cool things instead of replying instantly like she would've done if she'd been awake.

No, no, she wouldn't have. What was she talking about? As she slammed her fingers into the phone, she told herself she was super cool and busy and didn't have time to reply to texts the moment she read them.

Napping. Why? she replied, typing at the speed of light.

She tapped her phone impatiently despite only literally having sent the text. Serena sat up and pulled the cord of her lamp, and a dim red light filled the room, barely illuminating it at all.

She looked at herself in the mirror of her wardrobe. Her hair was a mess. Her tit was out again. She sighed and stepped out of bed, bare toes daintily touching the carpet as she pulled up her panties, which had fallen down her butt.

Serena had her phone securely in her hand as she poured a glass of water and opened the fridge, looking for something to eat. She scowled at its emptiness—just a can of cola and some condiments.

Her phone vibrated. She rushed to answer it, dropped it, and then, when reaching for it with her other hand, smacked it into the counter door.

"Fuck!" she cried, picking it up and was relieved her case had saved it.

Finished sacrificing a goblin to the nightqueen, then? Michael had texted.

I didn't give you my number, she replied. **Pretty sure this breaches some kind of law.**

There was a moment where she stared at her screen, willing it to beep a notification with her magic powers. *Three...two...one...now! Three...two...*then it finally came. *Yes, I knew I was magic!*

My bad, Michael said. **I had a bit to drink. See you at work tomorrow.**

Serena scowled. **How much have you drunk?** she said.

A couple of beers.

You're right. That is 'a bit.'

He did not reply. Because he was being respectful now. What a twat!

She decided to doubletext, thankful he didn't know how bad that was. **What you up to, anyway? Sitting in a sad bar?** She grinned at her goad. He was sure to take the bait of that one.

I wish! he replied.

She blinked. *Really? Two words? Is this all you're going to give me? You texted me!* She stared at her phone and resisted the urge to throw it against her wall.

Why am I getting so worked up about this? she wondered. *He's just some asshole who's bored, so he's texting the only person he knows.*

Are you being cryptic to fishhook me? she asked.

Fishhook? Is that a new social media? he replied.

Holy shit, you are annoying, she sent.

To that, he sent a flurry of emoji, tongues out, crazy eyes. Etcetera.

You text like an old person, she sent.

I am an old person, he replied.

I'm older than you.

You don't even know how old I am.

Serena snarled at her phone. **What are you doing, anyway?** she asked.

At the mansion of Lady Elowen. My brother works with her.

Fine, Serena replied. **Don't tell me.**

I am, look!

Serena received a picture of a marble-covered mansion. **That could be anyone's mansion,** she said. **Anyway, why text me? Shouldn't you be having fun?**

I am now, he replied.

Serena scoffed, rolled her eyes, and a faint smile of annoyance formed on her lips.

I'm going back to bed, she said, putting a stop to this nonsense before it got out of hand. Any moment now he would think they were actually friends or something.

Alright, he texted.

What? she replied. Holy crap. She was being fish-hooked. The asshole!

I just said alright? he texted.

A normal person would say goodnight.

Goodnight then. Have evil drow dreams!

You can't say that to me!
What you gonna do about it?

"Bah!" Serena squeezed her phone like a stressball, yanked open her fridge door, and was reminded she had nothing in it. She needed to order something.

Or she could go out to eat somewhere...with...

Calra. Yes. she'd see what Calra was doing.

That was totally the first person she thought of.

CHAPTER
SEVEN

TOMMY

Deep in the sewers of Stonereach, where darkgoblins roamed, and draugr bones clinked, the precious Pearl of Argon was lost for centuries, thrown away by a youthful princess. She'd gotten angry with her mother and decided to hide her augmented jewelry.

It was said to illuminate the dark for the wearer, and apparently it looked awesome, too.

It hadn't occurred to Tommy why the nobles hadn't sought it themselves, nor did it to the brutish bandits he partied with.

They scared him a little. There was Rogal, the orc. One of his tusks was cracked half off, and a milky eye bore a terrifying scar over it. Rogal was the muscle, their front line.

Wildro, the snakekin, hissed his words when he

spoke the common tongue. He was a spellshot, enchanting his bullets with deft casts of magic.

And then there was Brian. Brian grinned with bright white teeth and too many twinkles in both eyes, gently caressing the dagger on his hip.

Tommy avoided Brian as much as he could.

He was friendly. *Too* friendly. *And why wield a dagger in this day and age?*

Fortunately, they were so busy in their delving that they didn't have much time to interact. Tommy darted and weaved the traps, always first into danger. They called him their Leeroy. Tommy had no idea what that meant, assuming it was just a cool nickname.

Water dripped in the distance. Eternal flames flickered in a nonexistent wind, and an arched stone entranceway gave way to a dooming darkness.

"You're up, Leeroy," Brian said, batting him on the shoulder.

Tommy grabbed his peashooter—as Brian had called it—took a deep breath, ignored the terrifying nerves snaking in his stomach. He grabbed the torch off the wall and ran headfirst into the breach, where he yelled at the top of his voice.

About twenty drooling, droopy-eyed darkgoblins stared at him in surprise.

And hunger.

"Quite a lot of them this time!" he cried and ran back the other way, only to be toppled into by Rogal.

The big orc didn't even stop to help him back up. *So rude!*

As Brian and Wildro slithered past him—even though Brian was a human, it definitely felt like he slithered—Tommy pushed himself up, glad to have powerful warriors at his back. This was way better than with Michael. Michael cared way too much about safety. With these guys, Tommy got some real action and glory!

He felt a little bad about how much better he was doing now, though, so he'd been sure not to gloat about it to Michael when he saw him. Poor guy was sleeping on his parents' couch. Didn't he have his own place?

He also didn't understand why Michael traveled so far and wide when there were sewers and dungeons right here, underneath Stonereach.

Why the hells wasn't everyone raiding them all the time? Well, they'd had to sneak past the guards, of course, and all the closed-off walls. But that hadn't been hard. Brian had somehow taken care of all that. He'd just told the party to wait nearby and then alerted them all when he was done. He'd returned with a horribly bright smile.

Tommy was pulled back to the present.

"All done, Leeroy!" Brian called in that sinisterly sweet voice of his.

Tommy ran back to the group to witness the massacre they'd just enacted. One day, they'd teach him how to use a blade. He was glad that wasn't today, but he couldn't wait for it either.

"What's next?" Tommy asked. "Have we found the Pearl of Argon?"

Brian snickered. "Reckon it's in that chest," he said. "Be a good Leeroy and check it out, won't you?"

Tommy squinted. They were playing a trick on him.

"I will," he said. "Long as I get first dibs."

"Sure, sure, after everyone's had their dues paid first. Then you can get the pick of the lot." Brian had said this very quickly, so it must have been true. "Here," Brian said, handing over his knife handle first. "Jimmy the locks with this."

Tommy took the knife and crouched down before this unassuming chest, a smaller frame across a hard, dark wood. He put the point of the blade into the lock bolt and slammed down upon the handle, destroying the centuries-old mechanism that felt like it was just waiting for someone to finally complete what nature had started.

The next one opened just as easily. When Tommy turned back to the group. Brian gave him a thumbs up, and Wildro bared his teeth.

"Come on," Rogal grunted. "This bit's your job. We took care of the hard part. Go any slower, and we should maybe just swap jobs, and you can be the one to fight the monsters."

Tommy turned back quickly, flexed his fingers, and

then pushed open the chest with a whine. At first, a black void crept out of the ever-increasing gap, until he lifted the chest higher and pushed it to the edge of its hinges.

He stared inside the chest.

And something stared back.

SERENA

She stared up at the circular mirror which reflected towards the door. At any moment now, Michael was going to walk in, very hungover, and she would get to gloat. And then she would get to offer to go out to buy him something.

Wait, hadn't she already bought lunch? It was his turn.

But, but, but, if she did it, it would make her look awesome. He wouldn't think her a moody bitch then.

Or if he still did, at least he'd see that it wasn't intentional. It was in her blood, thanks to her mother. None of it was Serena's doing or responsibility at all, of course.

Thankfully, Serena wouldn't make the same mistake as her mother. That hypocrite cared so much about drow culture and then had gotten with her human father. That never softened her, apparently, according to some of the others Serena had asked. She still cared very much about being a good drow. It was only her father's insistence on letting her go off to study that her mother had relented.

But it wasn't your mother's fault you flunked, Serena thought. *Take some responsibility for your life for a change.*

She tapped her nail against the board, pulling at her skirt. She'd spent forever this morning choosing her outfit—a black and white plaid skirt, fishnet tights —obviously—and thigh-high black socks, with white stripes across the knees, a baggy blouse with a big neckline that ran across her chest but revealed none of her cleavage, and a choker with a ring at the front of the neck. To add some color, she'd worn her usual crimson spiky heart necklace that matched her eyes.

And the stupid idiot wasn't even there to see it. She'd wanted to walk in and watch his gaze travel up and down her body as he took all of her in, and then he'd pretend he wasn't doing it.

Serena sighed and picked up the duster, supposing she could get on with her responsibilities.

~

After about half an hour of work, the doorbell rang, and Serena snapped her gaze towards it, then quickly looked away so she didn't appear to have been doing just that.

But she frowned and looked again. Two police had

just walked in—a human male and a female lionkin, her fluffy ears poking out the sides of her hat.

"Serena Moonshadow?" the man asked.

She nodded, frowning as she got off the stool.

"We'd like to take you to the station to ask you some questions," the man said.

First, Serena touched her chest in confusion, and then her eyes widened in realization. "Is this about Patrick?" she asked.

"Let's just head to the station," he said bluntly. Serena looked to the lionkin, but her stony expression revealed nothing.

Serena immediately began picking at her nails.

I'd gotten away with it, she thought. *I mean. It was an accident. I thought they'd assumed it was an accident. It wasn't like I did it on purpose.*

Wasn't it?

"I've just got to lock up first," she said.

At that moment, the bell dinged, and one of the regular customers smiled and then paused when he realized the police were in the shop.

"We're closed," Serena explained, with an apologetic face, wracked with guilt.

That the police were staring at.

She quickly turned and went to the counter, the whole time under their watchful gaze. Her skin felt hot and heavy. Her boots were too tight against her feet. She needed to pull her sweater off, but she wore barely anything underneath, some skimpy crop top she would reveal when they closed the shop for lunch, to goad Michael into having a reaction.

Fuck.

~

"You do not have to say anything. But, it may harm your defense if you do not mention when questioned something which you later rely on in court. Anything you do say may be given in evidence."

Serena blinked at the words. The bright, blue bulb above her seared into her eyes. It was too bright. She rubbed her glasses as if cleaning them would make it any better. It didn't help.

She had no lawyer. Should she have gotten a free one? No, there was no evidence she'd done anything wrong.

Patrick would back that up when he woke up.

Oh fuck. Oh fuck. Oh fuck.

"I need a lawyer," she said. "A court-appointed one," she added.

The two interviewees sighed, rolled their eyes as they gave each other a look, and then one left to make arrangements.

He slammed a finger on the tape machine—making Serena jump—and then asked her to follow him to the waiting room.

After about half an hour, at which she tapped on her phone, she considered that she hadn't actually been arrested, merely asked to come in. That must have meant it wasn't completely serious, just a casual interview.

She had some missed calls from Michael. What was she supposed to say to him? *Sorry, can't come to work now, getting arrested under suspicion of trying to kill your uncle.*

It was an accident.

Keep telling yourself that.

She fell into her hands, rubbing her eyes underneath her glasses.

Soon enough, a woman arrived, with messy hair and glasses that magnified her eyes. She introduced herself as Sarah Badmen—a horrific omen if Serena had ever heard one.

The next twenty minutes were spent in a private meeting room, where they were allowed ten minutes to go over the situation. Serena explained that Patrick hated her and that it was a distinct possibility he may lie and claim she *had* tried to kill him.

As to why there was no security in the shop. Patrick didn't believe in that kind of thing because then it would capture all the dodgy dealings he'd been making, with *less-than-legitimately* obtained goods.

The interview went about as well as it could have. With them asking simple questions about what had happened and Serena relaying the events to the best of her memories. Patrick had tried to steady her, and she slipped, knocking the potion over—the *one* dangerous poison she herself was impervious to the effects of.

She'd tried to get a read on their expressions, but they were stony-faced as always. She'd tried to express her innocence, but her lawyer touched her arm to stop her.

And then eventually, she was free to leave, with a warning that she wasn't allowed to leave town until the investigation was over.

"It's a good result," Sarah Badmen said. "They don't feel they have enough evidence to arrest you."

"And then what?"

"Then, they'll question Patrick once he awakes, and hear his side of the story."

Serena rubbed her face, leaning over in defeat. "I am fucked," she groaned.

CHAPTER
EIGHT

MICHAEL

Sorry, the text read. Michael blinked at it in disbelief.

A leopard can't change its spots, he mused. **You're gonna need to send more than one-word texts,** he replied.

Not really sure how to say it to be honest. Can we close the shop and go for a walk or something?

Michael had only worked two days, and Serena wanted him to close the shop for two now.

I don't think Patrick would be very happy with us if we did that, he texted.

Fine, she said. **Do you mind if I take the day off?**

Michael's nose twitched.

"Okay if I get this?" a pretty voice said.

Michael was yanked out of the portal-like focus of his phone. He placed it under the counter, face down, as he served the nice lady—the catkin from the other day!

She flashed a warm smile and flicked her messy blonde hair out of her face. It kinda looked like a rat's nest—in an attractive way. Catkin never seemed to have neat hair, yet it never looked bad.

The blonde catkin had a necklace on, a long golden chain with a ring on the end, and as she played with it for a moment, placing it back between the crevice of her perky cleavage.

Michael's phone vibrated again, and his mind wondered about the message left on read.

"Thanks," Michael said, handing her the gauntlet and her change.

She smiled with brilliant white teeth.

"Have a great day," Michael added, smiling back but not with his eyes.

She seemed to sense it. Her smile turned into a scowl, and she turned and left, her tail swishing violently in her anger.

Back to the phone, he read the text from Serena. **Okay, fine, I'll come in.**

Take the day off, Michael replied. **Obviously, you don't want to tell me about what happened, but it sounds more serious than what usually bothers you.**

Sorry, she replied.

"I guess she's not coming in," Michael thought, feeling like a fool. A cute as heck catkin was standing before him, ready to flirt him to death—and probably more—but he was worrying about some moody goth and her endless problems.

Michael sighed and went to the back room, finding Patrick's diary to check if any relic hunters were due to arrive. The calendar was empty for several weeks, and the phone hadn't been ringing to give him updates, so truly, all there was to do was look after the shop.

So, as he sat at the counter, mindlessly scrolling through his phone, he was reminded why he had left the retail game in the first place. If you didn't own the store, it just wasn't worth it.

He did a little merchandising, making every item face the correct way, and then he did some dusting and washed the floors.

And then he did some being very bored.

"Sorry I'm late," Serena said, and Michael looked up with raised eyebrows, surprised to see her.

The place seemed so dull without her. Now, as she stood before him, it was like his favorite show just got a new episode. He never would have thought it, but having that drow around was incredibly entertaining.

Serena wore a loose skirt designed to look like the bottom was all ripped up. It revealed her knee on one leg and a little further up the thigh on another. Naturally, she wore some fishnet stockings.

Well, I know what to get her for her birthday, Michael thought.

Above, though, that was a little more surprising. It

was some kind of crop top blouse, the sleeves falling off both shoulders. At the center, crisscross ropes pulled together a loose diamond of her cleavage, showing two full crescents of her breasts. Underneath, her belly looked so cute. Michael thought it was awesome that she wasn't insecure about not having a completely flat stomach.

"Two things are eternal in this world," Serena said. "Me having a bad day, and you staring at my tits."

"They're not mutually exclusive," Michael replied. "And besides, they are...very on show right now."

"They are not!" She looked down and gave a sort of shrug. "Fair enough. Anyway, forget that. Don't you want to hear about what's bothering me?"

"That wasn't in the job description." Michael made a face of trepidation.

"Well, neither is working with your uncle's attempted murderer, but there you go." She crossed her arms.

"Excuse me?"

"The police came," Serena said, strolling casually to the counter, lifting the door, and standing before Michael. "They brought me in for questioning."

"You got arrested? They think you knocked those potions over on purpose?"

"Maybe, maybe not. I just got brought in for questioning. The potion that got him was from my lands, the only one I'd be unaffected by. Guess they thought it wasn't such a coincidence."

Michael considered the pretty half-elf. *I mean, sure,* he thought, *she totally looks like she's capable of heinous murder, but what drow doesn't? And a goth one at that.*

"But you'd be stupid to do that," Michael said. "You're the one that called the ambulance, and—"

"People do all sorts of stupid things when emotional, don't they? And thanks for not automatically assuming it was me."

"Didn't think long enough about it to tell you the truth. Frankly, I don't know you well enough to be rushing to your innocence. Hey, you're right. Why'd you try to kill my uncle?"

Serena reached over and gave his arm a gentle punch. "You're not funny."

Michael shrugged. "I have experienced danger all my life. Joking about it after is how I deal."

"Makes sense. I really didn't do it, though." She rubbed her temple. "You know how much I need this job."

"If you were guilty, I'd think you'd have been trying to act a little more innocent. If that catkin gets murdered tomorrow, they'll probably come looking for you for that as well."

"What catkin?" Serena cocked her head, and her crimson eyes stared through Michael's flesh.

"Oh, just this girl who keeps flirting with me. It's nothing."

"I see." Serena squinted. He could sense her insides

beginning to boil with the fist flickers of boundless rage.

"Do I need to be careful around the potions today?" Michael said, nervously chuckling.

Serena punched his arm again—gently, mind. She held elven strength in her blood, so she could have very easily hurt Michael without even trying.

"I would've let you have a day off if you told me this," he said.

"It seemed like something I shouldn't put in a text. What if they'd somehow twisted it around and...yeah." She rubbed her arm in the same place she'd punched Michael, and they just stared at one another for a moment, not really having much to say.

Michael snapped his fingers. "Do you know what you need?" he said.

"What?"

"A big burger."

"*Unf.*" Serena's eyes glazed over. Michael found it immensely satisfying.

"With cheese—melted," he added.

At that, Serena melted like the described food item.

"What else?" she asked, licking her lips.

"Well, all the usual trimmings—tomatoes, salad, diced onions."

"Go on..."

"And some sort of sauce, of course."

"You're turning me on."

Michael blinked. "It's just a burger."

"Fuck you. That was a joke!"

He grinned at her, and she smiled back. Then she looked away, removing her glasses to rub them, her messy ponytail swishing a little hypnotically.

"You know," she began. "I really didn't like you when I first met you."

Michael was learning to speak *Serena*. He wasn't quite fluent, yet he knew with certainty that meant: *I like you.*

Of course, it could have just been an act to get him on her side so that when the shit hit the fan with Patrick, he would declare she wasn't capable of doing such a thing.

∼

Serena rested her feet up on the counter, her jet-painted toes wiggling out of the rips of her tights. She bit into the burger, and her eyes rolled like she was having an extremely satisfying orgasm. She licked her lips, then her thumb where a little sauce had gotten on it. Her lips puffed out to fullness while her cheeks hollowed with a suckling motion.

"You're doing that on purpose," Michael said.

"It's just how I eat!"

"You eat like that around my uncle?" He raised his eyebrows. "That's really gross. He's twice my age."

Serena quickly pulled her legs back down to the

other side of the counter. "I really, *really* need you to know that I don't do that."

"I mean, he's no spring chicken, but he is closer to your age than I am."

"No, he's not! I'm only thirty. That's, like, a hot nineteen in half-drow years."

"A very hot nineteen," Michael said.

She squinted at him.

"Oh, so you can flirt with your body, but I can't flirt with my words? Double standards much."

"This is a complete abuse of power. I'm your employee!"

"It's a good thing you're not my secretary. You know, in actuality, I don't even work here. I've got no position. I might even be underneath you on the hierarchy."

"Oh you're definitely underneath me on the hierarchy." She bit her tongue, then her lips tightened, and she looked away. "Thanks," she said.

"Thanks for what?" Michael replied.

"Cheering me up."

"I didn't do anything."

"You did, and you did it when you're hungover, too."

"I only had like three beers last night."

"Yet you were texting me super embarrassingly."

"I was just using that as an excuse."

"An excuse for what?" Serena leaned forward on the counter, resting her chin on her palm. Her smile lit up the room. The glimmer in her eyes turned that light a sultry, warm orange. It was already like that, but somehow, Michael only noticed it then.

"An excuse to relinquish some boredom," Michael replied. "It's very boring around here without you causing trouble, you know."

"And that party was boring, too?"

"It was, actually. Real stuffy. Lots of CEO types talking about *synergy*. What in the hells does that even mean, anyway? Apart from what we've got going on right now."

"We do not have synergy!" Serena crossed her arms and huffed, then smirked. The smirk soon became a musical laughter. "I never thought I could enjoy working here. It's gonna be shit when you're gone."

Michael was so touched that he resisted actually touching his chest to express it. "Even if you did try to murder my uncle, and you're just saying such things to get me on your side during the trial, that's still one of the nicest things I've ever heard."

"You think there's gonna be a trial?"

"Will there be?"

"I don't know!" Serena put her head in her hands. "Your uncle seems like the type to pretend I did it on purpose."

"And now we're even further into 'I shouldn't trust you' territory." Michael walked over to the counter, standing above the upset drow.

She looked up at him and said, "Maybe it's just that, after that happened, I don't know. It feels like I can just say whatever now, and I don't need to worry about the consequences."

Michael cocked his head. "I may not have known you long, but you have *always* felt you can say whatever you want."

"No, I mean..."

"Mean what?"

"Nice things."

"Oh."

CHAPTER NINE

SERENA

"And he didn't ask you out? After all that?"

Sitting beside Serena on the couch, Calra sipped her coffee while her boyfriend, a big brutish troll named Clint, sat on the nearby chair, staring solemnly into the distance and sipping on his beer.

After Serena had told Calra she had important things to tell her, the two of them stopped to visit Serena, on their way out to a concert.

"That wasn't even what I wanted to tell you," she said. "He didn't ask me because...I sort of tried to kill his uncle."

"You *what?*"

"Well, not actually. But the police came and made me go in to answer some questions."

"Gods, like some kind of crime drama. Did you get a lawyer? I don't know if that was even a joke or not."

"I did actually! They appointed me one."

Calra shook her head. "Well, while I process all that, I have to say, it sounds like Michael didn't even consider you were capable of doing it."

"Still, there must be a tiny little inkling in the back of his mind. Hells, *I* even have one. I keep thinking that maybe I did it on purpose. Oh, Clint, you won't tell anyone all this, right?"

Clint grunted and came back to the realm. "What's that?" he asked. "Did you smash his brains in?"

Gods, they are really perfect for each other, Serena thought.

Clint grunted again and sat up a little. Something cracked in the seat, making Serena wince.

"Ask him," he said.

"What?" Serena gawped at Clint.

"Ask him, init. He's a bloke. Blokes like being asked."

Serena stared at the troll in disbelief. "No, they don't!" she said. "They want to be the one to ask. Otherwise, he'll get all...insecure about it. Like when a woman proposes. And I'm already a drow. He's probably heard all sorts of things about what we're like in the..." She glanced at Clint, not wanting to complete that sentence around him.

Clint grunted for a third time. "Ask him," he said. "Men like to be asked. Especially so when it's by someone we like. And he likes yer, you dumb drow. So stop this dumb school drama and just say what you think."

"I said what I thought all day to him! If he wanted to ask me, he would have."

"Maybe he's waiting for his uncle to get better so he can stop working at the store? Doesn't want to date someone he works with or something."

"Oh, that's such a good point, babe!" Calra said, rubbing Clint's forearm.

"Or maybe," Serena said. "He's not going to ask me because he's going back to his stupid evil job when he's finished at the shop, so there's no point."

Clint let out a slow, reverberant groan that vibrated the whole room.

"What is it, babe?" Calra asked.

"*Ask. Him. Tell him*! He can't read yer mind."

"I suppose it wouldn't be good to let all this hang in the air when we work together tomorrow," Serena said. "Although it might be—"

"Ask him!" Clint smashed his fist into the armrest, causing a crack. "Sorry," he said, rubbing his hand. "You lot are so frustrating! Expecting us to read your mind and then getting mad when we don't."

"My baby's so strong!" Calra kissed his knuckles. Serena tried not to retch at the saccharine sweetness.

Serena looked at the number in her inbox. She still hadn't saved him in her contacts. She sighed, pressed *ring*, and her heart thumped against her chest. She got up, walking from the living room to the hallway.

"Hello?" Michael said.

"Don't pretend you don't know who this is!" Serena spat into the phone.

Down the hall, Calra sighed.

"I mean, hi!" Serena said, far too brightly.

"Hello," Michael said again, this time with a little laughter.

"Do you know why I'm ringing?" she asked, then winced. She grabbed the heart-shaped pendant around her neck, and squeezed her fist around the spikes, letting them stab into her flesh, letting the pain punish her. It felt nice, too. *Oh gods, how is he going to contend with 'that' part of my drowness?*

"Is my car insurance out of date?" Michael asked.

"I hate you," Serena said, full of venom.

"Well, I still like the way you eat burgers."

Serena's heart swelled, a thousand butterflies fluttered in her chest.

"You should see how I eat them in bed," she said, full of sultriness, twirling a finger through her hair. Then, she became self-aware, scowled, and winced while Calra and Clint burst into laughter down the hall.

"Boy, you really want to sell me that car insurance," Michael said.

"I'm not good at this, okay!"

"I'm not so great at it either."

"Of course you are. That stupid catkin was ready to drink milk out of your hand."

"Common misconception. Cats don't drink milk."

"Umm, *ackshully*," Serena mimicked, putting on her nerdiest voice, "*cats don't drinksh milk.*"

"Also, I thought you didn't know who I was talking about when I mentioned her?"

"Are you going to ask me out or not!" she yelled, holding the phone before her mouth. "I mean, shut up. Don't say anything."

There was dead silence in the air, and in the living room, you couldn't even hear Clint's creaking on the chair.

"Wanna go on a date?" Serena asked.

"Oh *jeez*, I sure do!" Michael said in an awful nerdy kid's voice.

Across the realms, many wizards sensed a plane-shattering disturbance. High up in the mountains, several monks fainted. And somewhere in the lab, a scientist discovered a new element: *cringoniam*.

"That sounded funnier in my head," Michael said.

She could feel how red he had gotten through the phone. Serena herself had turned from purple to crimson to match her eyes.

Across the hall, in the faintest whisper as loud as the rock concert they were soon to attend, Calra said, "They're made for each other."

Serena closed her eyes and said down the phone, "I

want you to know I can only come when you use that voice."

She then quickly hung up.

~

MICHAEL

"What, the fuck, was that?" Wilson yelled, staring at Michael in disbelief.

"Me getting a date," Michael replied, staring at his phone in disbelief.

"Good on you," Wilson said, now moving past his brother's cringy dialogue. "When is it?"

"When is it...when is it...I have no idea."

Orla threw a cushion at Michael. "*You* should have asked *her*! Why did you make her ask?"

"I didn't make her ask. I just never asked her."

"I'd say you were playing it cool," Wilson began, "but we heard what you said to her."

Michael buried his head in his hands. "Why did I say all that? I never speak like that. What in the hells was I thinking?"

"I know what you were thinking," Orla sang.

The two men gazed at her.

"What?" Michael asked.

"Maybe it's best you find out for yourself," she said, getting up and strolling to the kitchen. Then she poked her head back in and said, "Call her back and arrange a date."

"Yes, ma'am."

She gasped. "Wilson, tell him right now he can never call me that."

"You can never call her that," Wilson repeated with a cheesy grin.

Michael sighed. "Maybe I'll just text her," he said.

When you free? he texted.

"Nice," Wilson said, giving a thumbs up. "Very decisive."

"What's that?" Orla called, putting her head back in the room.

"He just asked her when she was free."

"Michael!"

"Oh, my gods," Michael cried. "I cannot wait to get back on the road. It was better when skeletons were trying to kill me. At least they didn't scold me as they did it." He grinned to let her know he was joking. "Go on then, what did I do wrong this time?"

"Tell her the date and time you'd like to meet! She can decide if she's free or not."

Michael's phone vibrated. "Too late," he said.

Dunno. When you free?

"See!" Orla said.

"See what?" Michael frowned. "Why is this so difficult? It used to be so easy before."

"*I know why*," Orla sang again.

"You should meet her and become friends. You're both infuriating."

"Oi, that's my wife!" Wilson said.

"Thank you!"

"Right," Michael said, standing up for no reason. "I'm just going to ask her. Tonight. It has to be tonight."

Tonight, drinks? he asked.

Yes, she replied, before Michael had even hit enter.

"Must've been a phone error," he mused. "By the way, she may have tried to kill Uncle Patrick."

"Oh, who hasn't tried to kill Uncle Patrick," Orla hummed.

"I'm serious," Michael said. "The police questioned her."

"And now you're going on a date with her?" Wilson frowned, the seriousness of it seeming to catch up to him as he turned the TV off and sat forward, rubbing his chin. "Why didn't you say anything?"

Michael shrugged. "She was the only one who saw what happened. Seems normal they'd want to question her. They let her go right after. Who's to say they even suspected her of anything?"

"Gods," Wilson said. "You better get in there before she heads off to jail, then."

"That's terrible, Wilson!" Orla sighed, shaking her head.

CHAPTER TEN

MICHAEL

Sports blasted out of the TV above the bar. Michael had half a mind to ask them to turn it to a rock music station or something. He looked around the bar wondering if it was divey enough, or too divey? Should he have gone for a restaurant?

He swallowed. *Commit,* he told himself. *It doesn't matter where you meet. She's dating you, not the bar.*

No, she's going on 'a' date with you. She's not dating you.

He shook his head and resisted the urge to get a beer. If anything, Serena would need to drink more than him just to keep up with him. He had to be careful of that. She'd mentioned once that she could drink far more than the average man, and not even in an 'I drink a lot' way. Just because of her drow lineage.

Michael checked his sleeves were at the appropriate level of rolled up, checked he didn't have any stains on his favorite flannel shirt, checked his phone, checked it again, checked it a third time, and then ordered a bag of peanuts. "Just waiting for my date to arrive," he explained, so the bartender didn't think he was lingering there for the free seat.

"That her?" the bartender asked.

Michael swiveled in his chair. His jaw immediately hit the floor.

Serena wore a green velvet dress, more gothic in the historical sense than a fashionable goth. It had a deep, plunging cleavage with flowery patterns across the line, dancing across where her tits were pushed mercilessly together like two plump fruits ready to be squeezed until they exploded with drow juice.

She wore long-sleeved gloves that went up past her elbows, some kind of shiny leather. But, as if to remind him of what she usually dressed like, her Dick Marvin boots stomped along the ground, one of the laces undone.

Her hair was down, all to one side and wavy, nearly hiding one of her pointy ears, the tip just poking out. White stripes ran down the black waves like celestial ribbons upon a night sky.

What she was wearing—minus the boots—did not suit the bar one bit. She'd overdressed in the best way anyone could ever overdress.

"Yeah, that's her," Michael said, unable to believe that it actually was her.

The bartender made no comment, perhaps wise. Or maybe he was just as speechless as Michael was.

Serena smiled, and he realized then she wasn't wearing her glasses. Her crimson eyes gleamed under the lights of the bar. In the dim old bar, she looked very much like she'd stepped out of the past.

"You look amazing," Michael said.

She just smiled. He expected her to say something like 'You didn't make an effort.' All she did was blush in her cheeks and sit down beside him. He realized she might've just applied blusher, because the red stayed, and it looked very pretty, as did the wild dash of black mascara.

Her thighs fattened mercilessly when she sat down, her bodacious behind a perfect curve against the seat.

Michael tried not to stare, but she just smiled when she saw him look all over her.

"You have permission," she said. "Not that you haven't already taken it." Then she said to the bartender, "Wine glass of vodka, please."

Serena squinted at Michael. He felt he was being tested.

"Sorry, did you just—" the bartender began.

"You heard me," Serena said, though with a polite tone. Michael swore he could hear the faint hint of annoyance that came from having to say the same thing over and over, though she certainly had been polite.

"Michael," she said, leaning closer.

A cloud of sensual perfume enveloped him, and he gazed into the little texture of her full, red lips, matching her eyes perfectly.

"Yeah?" he said.

"*Yeah*," she mimicked, then gently brushed his arm. "You being so nervous is putting me at ease, you know."

"I'm not nervous!" he said, way too loudly, to the raised eyebrow of the bartender. "Beer, please," he said.

"Anyway," Serena said. "Could we sit somewhere a little more private? I don't like it when people can hear my conversations."

Michael stood up, and Serena gracefully left her chair, slotting her hand inside his arm. She smelled wonderful, intoxicatingly so.

"Don't make a thing of it," she said, squeezing it.

"I thought that was the whole point," Michael replied, as they strolled off to a dark booth in the corner. One low, hanging bulb cast a wide wash of dim orange light, a chain holding the dusty blue and gold glass lampshade.

"I mean," Serena began, biting her lip. "Okay fine. Just not *too* big a thing."

"Are you playing games with me?"

They sat down on either end of the table, a new

barrier between them. Serena sipped her drink, looking away, and then she glanced up again. She wasn't wearing her glasses. Did she have contacts in?

"I'm not trying to play games with you," Serena finally said. "That's the point."

Michael leaned back, studying the drow. "When was the last time you dated?" he asked.

"A long time ago," she replied. "You?"

"A long time ago."

"You've been with women, though."

"It's not really the same."

"Why not?"

"If I said why, you'd accuse me of 'making a big thing of it.'"

Her nose twitched. "You can look at my tits if you want."

Michael laughed, sipping his beer. "Does saying that make it easier?" He purposely looked into her crimson eyes, though his periphery feasted on the blurry treat of her swollen mounds.

She nodded. "Aren't people supposed to talk about like, work? Friends? Family history? That sort of thing."

"Yes, when you're just meeting the person. We already know each other."

"We've hardly more than just met."

"Sixteen hours is a long time, in a way."

"I suppose you're right."

"*I suppose you're right*," Michael imitated.

"Shut up!" Serena whacked his arm, smiling. "Now tell me how good I look."

"You already know how good you look," he replied.

"I like it when you say it."

"Shame it's not reciprocated."

"Men don't need to be told they look good. They just need their dick grabbed."

Michael laughed. "That's very much not true. Did you know most men are so starved of positive attention a simple 'you look nice' will carry them through the week?"

"Clint said something like that."

"And Clint is?" Michael squinted. He felt a surge of jealousy he was only half ashamed of.

"Calra's boyfriend." Serena sipped her drink, and the edge of her boot brushed against Michael's thigh.

Michael sighed in relief. "And *Calra* is?"

"My best friend."

"That's nice."

"*That's nice*," Serena imitated. "That's what you sound like. *That's nice*."

Michael shook his head in disbelief, putting his arm on the chair and looking around the bar.

"Something more interesting going on?" she asked.

"It's nice you have a friend," Michael said.

"Surprised?"

"Pleasantly so."

"Yeah." Serena sipped her drink. "I'd be surprised, too."

"Take a day off," Michael said in exasperation.

"A day off?"

"You know, from—" Michael motioned up and down. "—all that attitude. You think you don't deserve to be happy or something? Even unhappy people deserve a night off, now and again."

"Are you happy?" Serena asked.

Michael turned his lips to the side and then drank a lot of beer. "I suppose I haven't thought about it," he finally said.

Some kind of crooning jazz music rang out in the bar. It sounded like how cigarettes tasted.

"All that running into tombs," Serena said, with a sly smile, "just what are you running from?"

"Standing in one place and finding nothing there, perhaps," Michael replied.

"Oh."

"What?"

"I didn't actually expect you to answer." Serena smirked in some kind of victory. She looked so cute when she smirked. Like a naughty little elf—one with massive tits, of course.

"Well, you did ask," Michael said.

"I didn't know men talked like that. Drow men certainly don't."

"Maybe they do amongst women who allow them to. Or does that change the way you see me?"

"Yes." Serena sipped her drink for an agonizingly long time, staring through him. "For the better," she finally added. "Perhaps you take what isn't yours to fill that big, vast, empty hole inside."

"I could fill it with your tits just fine."

"A defense mechanism." Serena raised her eyebrows. "Crudeness to deflect the loneliness."

"You're the one usually doing that," Michael replied. "I learned it from you."

"Well..." Serena ran a finger around her wine glass, making it ring.

She snarled and rolled her eyes but could not fake that lingering smile. The crimson red was perfectly applied across the lines of her full lips, lips that must have come from the human side of her. Elves were usually svelte, waifish. Petite—not words that could be used to describe Serena. She was one of a kind.

"What?" she asked, scowling.

"Just thinking about how good you look."

Serena laughed, then fished into her handbag to put on her glasses. "There, now I can see how good *you* look. Very handsome. Like some adventurer out of a pulp novel. Do you wake up with your hair all swept like that, or do you spend hours in the mirror every morning?"

"There's only one way to find out."

"What would you make me in the morning, for breakfast?"

"What would *you* make me?" Michael challenged.

"I asked you first."

"*I asked you first,*" Michael imitated.

It seemed like Serena was going to smack his arm, but instead, she slotted her fingers around his palm.

"That copying thing is *so* annoying," she said. "Who the hells started that anyway?"

"Let's agree never to do it again." Michael turned the handhold into a handshake.

They shook hands and laughed, then their fingers slotted into each other and rested on the table. It felt ceremonial as they both looked at their hands and laughed again, giving them a little tremble.

"Maybe we should hold hands under the table," Michael said.

Serena bounced her eyebrows.

Michael rolled his. "For someone who hasn't dated anyone in a long time, you are quite filthy, aren't you." He shook his head.

"If you call my bluff, I'll scream," Serena said.

Michael let go of her hand and stood up.

"What are you doing?" Serena looked genuinely scared, eyebrows raised and eyes wide as Michael walked over to her side of the table.

Then, just as he was about to climb into her side, he turned tail and strolled toward the bartender.

"Another round of drinks, please," he said to him. "And some cheesy nachos, loaded with all the trimmings."

"Sure thing," the bartender said. "Date going well?"

Michael nodded. "Yeah." His cheesy smile revealed

the true answer. "And, can you...change the music?" He grabbed some notes from his wallet and put them in the tip jar. "Rock? Oldschool rock? Got that?"

"Aye, we do."

Moments later, Michael returned to the booth with his drinks, watched intently by Serena, who had crossed one leg over the other, mercilessly fattening her thighs. He wanted to bite into it, taste the purple-tint of her flesh. Maybe even get gross and lick it.

Michael sat beside her, her thigh brushing against his as he passed over the drink.

"Your phone went off," she said, glancing at it face-down on the table.

"So?" Michael replied.

"Might be important."

"I can check it later."

She smiled, still sipping her drink. "I really didn't need a second one—" Suddenly, the sad jazz music turned into a guitar riff. "You did that?"

"I've got sway in this city. I'm a big cheese."

"Sure." She grinned at him. Her smile wouldn't falter. "So, work will be awkward tomorrow."

"Or awesome," Michael replied.

"It already was today." Suddenly, Serena's stomach rumbled. Her cheeks flushed a slightly deeper shade of red. "So what are you planning on doing," she asked, "you know, after Patrick recovers?"

Michael shrugged. "See if he's got any jobs planned for me. I couldn't find anything in the diary, though he tends to keep a lot private in his head, in case the wrong eyes find it."

"Something super illegal and disrespectful to some dead culture."

"A culture too dead to complain about it. Do you really care? Or do you just pretend to care because you think it's the right thing to do?"

Serena blinked at him. "Of course I care!" she said, then glanced away slightly, drinking a bigger gulp.

"I think you care too much about far too many things, and if you stopped for a moment, you might consider what is really important in your life."

"Oh yeah, like what?"

"I dunno." Michael shrugged. "Figured I'd come up with something by the end of the sentence."

Serena twitched her cute nose. "Maybe because nothing's important," she said. "We're all gonna die a horrible death someday, so we might as well care about things while we're still alive. Those people you steal from are dead, but we're alive. I'm not really sure what point I'm trying to make, to be honest. You should just kiss me to shut me up."

"You kiss me." Michael leaned a little back.

"I asked you on the date, so you've got to kiss me. It's a fair trade."

Michael laughed, then leaned a little forward, staring at her lips.

"Nachos!" a waitress said, placing them on the

table. Michael and Serena cleared their throat and thanked her, and then she finally left.

"You got me food?" Serena said, going doe-eyed.

"Sure, I was hun—"

Her mouth crashed against his. She grasped his shirt and smushed her lips into his, and her scent enveloped him, as did several thousand butterflies inside him. He'd kissed women before. Why did this feel different?

They broke the kiss.

"You're easy to please," Michael said, a little breathless.

"I really, *really* am not," Serena replied, smiling as she ran her fingers through his hair.

They began eating the terrible yet oh-so-satisfying nachos while Michael grabbed his phone to check who'd been calling him, hoping—and guiltily *not* hoping—it was Patrick on the mend.

Hey bro, Wilson said. **Tommy's not come home the past two nights. You hear from him?**

Michael frowned, then texted, **Nah. He not answer his phone?**

No signal, Wilson replied. **Maybe he's on a long expedition, but he always checks in. It's not like him.**

Michael wasn't sure what he was supposed to do in this situation. **Is there anything I can do?** he asked. He could feel Serena reading over his shoulder, and reached under the table and took her hand, which she squeezed supportively.

I don't know, Don't you have some contacts? Find out who he was party'ed up with?

"How do you not know?" Michael said aloud in disbelief. "You don't have to be a helicopter parent, but you could at least know who your son hangs out with."

Serena squeezed his hand a little tighter, and then a crunch of nachos was very loud in his ear.

I'll see what I can do, Michael texted. **Will get back to you as soon as I hear something.**

"Sorry," Michael said, to Serena.

"Go ahead. I'm not going anywhere." Serena touched the cheek facing away from her, pulled him close, and planted a soft kiss on the one closest to her.

Michael dialed some numbers and spoke to some fences and fixers he knew, but most of them had not even heard of Tommy. Others thought he was still working with Michael.

"How the hells can nobody know what he's doing? He's been out raiding. Surely one of them must know." Michael sighed, texted Wilson to say that he hadn't heard anything, and dug into the nachos.

"Maybe you should be with your family," Serena said.

"It wouldn't help. I'm doing everything I can *here*."

Michael then sent another text, suggesting they go through Tommy's room to see if there were any clues they might find, and they replied that they'd already done that.

"What do you need?" Serena asked. "Can I help?" She rubbed his arm affectionately.

"A distraction," Michael said.

"I can do that." She grabbed his arm and put it around her, sighing as she rested on him. She placed her hand on his chest. It felt like a sacred key slotting perfectly into the lock.

Michael tapped on the table.

"You still bothered about it?" Serena asked, raising her head to gaze at him.

"I shouldn't have checked my phone," he said.

"Fine," Serena replied. "Let's look for him properly, then." She gulped down her glass of vodka, and Michael thought she resisted a belch. "Come on. I've got a laptop at my place. Let me just delete my history first so you don't see all the freaky shit I look at."

They made to leave, but then Serena stopped, pulling his arm back. "What?" Michael asked. "Are you nervous about taking me to yours? We don't have to do anything. Like you said, we're just looking for Tommy."

"No, it's not that," she said. "I just want to bring the nachos."

CHAPTER ELEVEN

SERENA

Serena wondered if it was terrible to think that she was sort of...glad Michael's nephew was missing.

No, she wasn't. That was horrible. What she meant was that she was glad they had a goal they could focus on together, a problem to solve. They were too combative when faced with one another. Too spicy.

She liked it, she *did* like it, but what would happen when the novelty wore off for him, and she was just some angry drow that gave him headaches?

She squeezed his arm tighter, as they walked through the city streets, warm city lights guiding their way. The store was closed tomorrow, so they'd have all night to look, and he'd have no excuse to leave tonight to get an early night.

It was too soon for all that. It wasn't...time yet. Wasn't it?

Fortunately, they had to find his nephew.

"What's wrong?" Michael asked.

"Nothing," she said.

"You keep huffing."

"I do not huff."

"Fine. Why do you keep not huffing?"

"Overthinking, as per usual."

"About us?"

"No, about when the DLC to Elven Ring will be released. I've been waiting forever."

Michael grabbed her hand instead, and their fingers interlocked as they approached her apartment.

"You're gonna overthink and come up with problems no matter what happens between us," Michael said, stopping in the middle of the street.

"I'm glad you see me like that." Serena arched her neck up to gaze at his stupid, handsome face.

He ran his fingers through her hair, gently touching her skin. Then, they trailed up to her ear, gently brushing the point and teasing the sensitive nerves there.

"Do you know what that means?" Serena gasped. "You don't just...touch an elf there."

"What I meant by what I said was," Michael began, seeming to ignore her, "if you're going to overthink no matter what happens, then do what you want and accept the feeling. Would you rather have what you want and feel bad, or not have it, and feel worse?"

"I'd rather not feel bad at all. Also, we need to find your nephew."

"He's probably in a dungeon somewhere battling skeletons, and the world will have to go on after we find him."

"Let's just see how we get on, then." Serena smiled at him a little weakly. "This is only our first date, after all."

"Does that mean I'll get a second?"

Serena loved how hopeful he looked.

"It means *I'll* get a second," she said.

They carried on the journey, finally making it to Serena's apartment complex, where she shakily tried to shunt the key in the door, dropped it, and then was a little grateful she got to give Michael a view of her bending over. Her butt may have been way too big, but for some reason, Michael liked that about her. She was more than happy to show it to him, especially the way it fattened out more when she bent her knees and pushed the balls of her feet against her buttcheeks.

Serena turned back to gaze up at him, running her fingers through her hair. "You make me feel like some kind of, I don't know." She shook her head in disbelief. "Why do I like it when you perv on me?"

"I don't perv on you," he replied, convincing no one.

"Well, whatever you're not doing, keep not doing

it." She took his hand and led him toward the elevator. Then, she sensually walked backward inside, pulling him along and biting her lip, hoping to symbolically imply she wanted him inside her.

"You just used my nephew as an excuse to get me in here." Michael's breath tickled her ear, making her shudder as he nipped on it. *He shouldn't do that. He shouldn't touch me there. How does he not know what that means?*

And yet, he continued to nibble on her ear like a rabbit chewing leaves, but in a hot way.

Serena's hand trailed down his chest.

Michael brushed the back of his knuckles upon the side of her neck, to her chest, above her breasts. He was just brushing, exploring, making her warm.

"Have you ever been with a drow?" she asked.

"No," he said. It felt like an admittance.

"Do you know about *us*?"

"A little," Michael said. "But mostly what rumors say, and you know how off the mark they can be."

"How we're all evil, devilspawn, untrustworthy, keen to watch the world burn?"

"Well, that."

"Half-truths. Depends on the drow. That isn't really what I referred to, though."

Suddenly, the elevator dinged, and Serena took his hand to walk him down the hall, though he swiftly walked beside her. When they finally got to her door, she felt his gaze eating her as he pushed open the door to her apartment.

She turned and threw herself at him but was suddenly stopped by his hand on her chest.

"Let's wait," he said, swallowing. The tendon in his neck flexed hypnotically, she wanted to bite it.

"What sort of man are you!" she scowled, swiping his hand away to push herself up against him, letting her tits smush him very purposefully, but resting her head on his chest as he stroked her hair. It sent waves of calm through her body.

She felt safe in his arms.

"We should find your nephew," she said. "As we planned."

He continued stroking her hair, pressing his nose into it to take a tremendous long sniff, making her shudder with warmth. A hardness pushed up against her, a tightness in his jeans begging for her to release, for her to...

"Coffee?" she asked.

"I'd love one."

"It's in the kitchen!" She pushed off him and ran down the hall, not before taking a glance back at the throbbing length in his jeans. *Lucky me,* she thought, heating up between her thighs.

"I don't even know where the kitchen is!" Michael called.

Good, she thought. *That will give me a chance to delete the super weird search history on my laptop.*

"You'll figure it out!" she said. "It's a small apartment."

She threw herself on the couch, grabbed the laptop, and set to delete all of the perverted erotica about adventurers, specifically the search history where she'd typed *'adventurer x evil drow'*. Surprisingly, she had found about twenty. *Praise the gods for Twotpad.* If it was a physical book, her favorite scenes would have had bent, wet-stained pages.

"Found it," Michael called.

She hurried and hit delete, then began typing into the address bar, but the words still came up. "Cunting fuck," she muttered, then changed *'delete weekly'* to *'delete from now until the beginning of time, including before you even had the damn idea in the first place.'*

"Wanna make it a fun coffee?" she asked down the hall, leaning over the couch and then slipping over, slamming on her butt.

"I don't think we're supposed to be having fun right now," he said. "What was that?"

"Nothing!" She climbed back on the couch, pulled her dress back over her butt, and then pulled off her shoes so he could look at her cute feet. Maybe she would put them on his lap, ever so gently brushing against the erection she planned to make him permanently suffer for the duration of his stay—or, until he got so pent up he did something about it.

Heheh, he's gonna rail me so fucking hard, she

thought. *I hope he can't contain himself and comes inside me after a few furious pumps, then gets all embarrassed and I can act super caring and understanding and explain that the first time doesn't count, it's a freebee, a trial run for the main event, and then he will literally think I am best girl and then fuck me mercilessly untill I'm sore and bowlegged.*

"And yes," Michael called, "I do want to make it a fun one. What'd you mean by that?"

"There's whiskey in the cupboard," Serena said, fluttering herself.

"Ah."

Serena then lay on her side, resting on her elbow, making her curves extra curvy. She ran her fingers down them, then realized they were trying to look for his lost nephew, so sat up just in time for Michael to enter the room, carrying the lovely steamy cups of coffee.

He passed one over, then sat beside her, and then she noticed him admiring her TV. "Who needs to go outside when you've got one as big as that," he said.

"Indeed," Serena replied, glancing at his crotch. "Anyhoo." She scooched beside him, placed the laptop on their mutual laps, and suggested he start trolling through the kid's social media to see what he'd been posting.

"I don't have social media," Michael said.

"Of course, you don't," Serena replied, liking that about him. *That means he wouldn't be spending all his time looking at photo-manipulated supermodels. By the gods what is wrong with me?*

"You seem pleased about that," Michael said.

"Can't have you spending all your time looking at photo-manipulated supermodels," she said, committing to it fully because she wanted to see what he'd say.

Serena sipped on the coffee while he mused on the words with a bemused smile, but he didn't say anything at all. So, Serena logged into her *Grimoirefriends* account, and Michael told her Tommy's full name.

But it was private.

Soon enough, they had the login for his brother Wilson's account, and were trawling through his friends and posts to try and find some clue of what he'd been getting up to.

"Kids these days don't talk on each other's walls," Serena explained. "It's all in private chats. We could post on his wall, though, asking if anyone has any information about his whereabouts?"

"Sounds good," Michael said.

"I hope you find him," Serena said. "That sounds dumb to say. His parents must be worried sick."

"Mmm," Michael said. It was a very manly way to say there was something on his mind without saying it.

"What's up, babe?" Serena asked, then covered her

mouth. "Sorry, I mean, what's up, dude?" She winced. "This is all your fault for coming here."

"You invited me!" Michael gave a sigh that said, *here we go again.*

Yet Serena couldn't help herself. "You should have just given me a kiss good night, so I could go home all hot and heavy, ready for you to come up on our second or third date!"

"But we're here to look for my nephew," Michael said. "It's not like I'm touching you or anything."

Then, at that grand moment, his hand slipped under the laptop, grasping her thigh in a squeeze that warmed her and got her a little wet. Fortunately she didn't flood the laptop, because it dropped to the floor in a crash.

"Oh fu—" he began, but Serena threw her thigh over him and straddled him, slipping her tongue between his lips as she ground against his emerging erection.

She tasted the hot coffee on his breath, and the whiskey. It would've been gross on anyone but him. With him, she relished the taste.

Michael stroked Serena's cheek and gazed into her eyes. It seemed like he could look through her and see all her pain and suggest it didn't matter anymore.

She didn't even feel pain anymore, just red, hot, lust, and several other odd feelings she hadn't recalled feeling before. If she put it into words, it would surely send him running for the hills. She'd only known him a few days!

Eighteen hours, thirty minutes, and two seconds, but who's counting?

"I can't promise I'll reign myself in," she said. "But I promise I'll try." She shoved her tongue in his mouth again, and something vibrated on her crotch. "I'd rather we didn't use that," she began.

"It's my phone, you dumbass," he said.

She slipped off him, hand trailing down to stroke against his crotch, feeling the hardness begging to be relaxed. He spread his legs like some giant dragon's wingspan, and she looked at his thighs and imagined them pounding into the back of her legs. She imagined his big cock stretching and stuffing her oh so tiny slit and—

"What?" Michael said on the phone. "Are you sure? Maybe it's just a coincidence. I'll check now and call you back."

Michael picked up the laptop and typed with two individual fingers because, of course, he was the slowest typer in the world.

The first letter was *a*, and auto-complete showed *'adventuring man x evil drow thotpad'.*

Serena froze in shock. He continued typing the word *'adventuring'*, and the search stayed there for an eternity.

Finally, he completed the search. *'Adventuring party slain in dungeon.'*

Serena's heart sank for him. "Oh, Michael..." she felt genuine hurt for what he may be feeling. This surprised her, not that she felt it, but what *it* felt like. It wasn't some fabled feeling in a story. It churned at her insides.

Michael clicked on the article. "Three men were brutally slain in a dungeon attack last night," he read, then showed the pictures of a human male with a creepy smile, an orc, and a lizardkin. Michael sighed in relief, and Serena sighed doubly so for him. "Tommy is dumb, but he's not dumb enough to hang out with the likes of these." Michael then whistled. "Says they were torn to shreds, heads ripped clean off. The darkgoblins surrounding them were all dead too, in more usual ways, so it must have been something else. All they found was some open chest—Anyway, who cares about that?"

He clicked back on his brother's social media, and many people had commented on the post asking about Tommy's whereabouts, and none of it seemed very helpful.

"Can we watch something?" Michael asked. "I wanna take my mind off this for now."

"Sure!" Serena said, feeling a little too happy about that, as he put his arm under her, and she rested underneath him, still burning behind her panties but understanding why he was no longer in the mood.

"That was an interesting search history," Michael

said as Serena flicked through the channels absent-mindedly.

"Women read smut, okay!" she yelled. "It's totally normal."

"Smut? No, I wasn't talking about that one."

"What..." Serena's eyes widened. *Oh fuck. What had he seen?*

She turned the TV off and slipped down the couch, then slithered between his legs, spreading them by stroking down his thighs.

"What are you doing?" he asked.

"Obviously I'm not looking for my keys," she said, running her hands over the hard bulge between his legs. She could feel its need. She wanted it in her mouth, to feel that salty taste and his power throbbing against her tongue.

And she was trying to distract his mind from the horrible search he'd seen.

Whatever it was, it was likely more of a third-date discussion.

CHAPTER
TWELVE

MICHAEL

"Get up," Michael said, pulling her back to the coach.

"Mommy horny, Michael," Serena said with an over-the-top pout.

"Oh gods, please never say that again."

Serena put her head on his lap and threw her arms out, stretching her feet and wiggling her toes. The black nail varnish glimmered under the dim ceiling light like ten little jets.

Michael rested his hand on her stomach. She felt nice to his touch. Serena beamed up at him and didn't seem to mind one bit that his erection throbbed against her head, twitching like it was banging on the cage of his jeans.

He rubbed her ears, and her eyes rolled.

She threw off her glasses and rubbed her face. "You

can't...do that!" she said, trembling like she was coming over in pleasure.

Her dress felt like the smoothest silk. The back of his knuckles glided over her stomach, tracing the lines up to the curve of the other breast.

Then Michael got up, and she slammed a fist onto the couch.

"What is this torture!" she spat, sitting up and crossing her arms.

Michael went to the kitchen, found the bag of nachos, and began plating them up, making a jingling sound that had her cry, "Ooh!" because she knew exactly what it was.

He brought it in, and she rubbed her hands together in joy, her tits jiggling mercilessly as she did so.

"Are you drunk?" Michael asked.

"Jusshst a liffle bit," she said over the top as she crunched away on the nachos. Something about her blossoming into delight when she ate really pleased Michael. "Why don't you wanna *fug* me?" she asked, through a mouth full of food.

"I feel a bit guilty about it with Tommy missing. Something keeps nagging at me about it."

"Oh good, I thought it was something I'd done."

"Well, this was only supposed to be a date."

"Maybe we just *need* each other," she said, staring into his eyes. The air stilled with meaning, broken by the crunch of a nacho.

"You are a naughty brat," Michael said in some fabled attempt to save grace.

Serena froze, the chip hovering before her mouth. She put it down, then put the bowl down on the ground and threw herself over Michael's lap, placing her butt right below his head.

"What are you doing now?" Michael asked, his hand resting on her juicy butt, squeezing the tender flesh, hypnotized by its squishiness.

"You called me a brat!" she said, pushing her butt out more. "Brats need..."

Without thinking, Michael peeled her dress back to reveal the lovely lilac flesh of her buttocks. A black thong disappeared between the fat cheeks. His cock surged against her groin, and she giggled, rubbing against it.

"I'm a drow," she said. "Once you shake the bottle, don't be surprised when it explodes."

Serena rested her head on her forearms, a big smile on her face as she closed her eyes.

What was Michael to do but give in to her wishes? He flattened his hand, and a *smack* rang out, making her tremble in delight as her butt jiggled from the impact. It wasn't usually his sort of thing, but it could be.

"Are all drow like this?" he asked.

"Filthy sex perverts? Sure. I'm a little different, though."

"How?" Michael spanked her again, the shot rang out of the apartment, and Serena cried out in pleasure.

Then she turned around and sat up, saying, "The drow side of me wants you to...do awful things to me."

"And the human side?"

"Wanted me to wait until I found someone I actually wanted to do it to me." Serena bit his ear, nibbling like he had done to her. Her warm breath tickled into his ear as she whispered, "Let's get it out of our system, then we can focus properly on the problem. I'll help you however I can."

Michael nodded, losing blood in his mind as he said, "Get it out of your system then." He laid back, putting his arm over the crouch, ready to see what she would do.

She smiled, sat up, and slipped off the shoulders of her emerald green dress. Her bosom seemed to heave, and she pulled it further down, peeling it off the curvy mounds to reveal a see-through, sheer-like bra, her deep purple nipples clear to see, their points smushed against the fabric.

Her gaze lazily quested for his crotch as her fingers ran over it. "Maybe," she said, closing her eyes as she stroked on his cock, and waves of pleasure shot through his body like a string behind his navel being plucked to make a melodious song.

"Maybe what?"

"Maybe we can keep it simple tonight? I'm already rushing you, so I can at least...keep it simple for now."

"Simple—meaning?" Michael kept catching his own breath, staring at the beauty of her tits.

"You know, nice stuff."

Michael nodded. "Nice is good." He leaned over and kissed her neck, taking long, deep breaths of her scent. She continued to rub at him, tracing his shape through the jeans, while he kissed all over her chest, then found the clasp and, with all the deft expertise of one who dealt with sensitive traps, unhooked the bra in one fell movement.

Serena slipped the bra down her shoulder, then sat on her knees, her emerald dress a puddle around her hips, her curvy figure like some goddess statue, all eloquently fallen, voluptuous, and cuddly looking.

Michael's mouth was dry. He swallowed past a great lump in his throat as he cupped her hefty bosom. Her nipples felt tender to his touch, then hardened against his thumbs.

Serena gasped, fumbling with his jeans to unhook the button. The zipper sliding down sounded like lightning in his mind. He helped pull them down, and his boxers came with it, springboarding his cock up, making her jump a little in surprise.

Serena dove down, the tips of her long flowing hair tickling over it briefly, before she swept it away to let the black-and-white hair flow like a waterfall between his legs, then off the couch.

Her fingers grasped around his cock, stroked gently, and she planted lovely little kisses against the underside, each one sending tiny surges of pleasure through him, swelling behind his navel in desperate urges of release he held back.

Those little kisses turned into longer licks. She slid her tongue up at him, then frowned and gave it a wipe with her thumb.

"Got a bit of nacho chips on it."

Michael burst into laughter. "You are ridiculous." He could not have been more fond of her.

She smiled, reached over to take a big gulp of coffee, swirled it, and drank it.

"Nothing like a bit of sensual coffee," Michael joked. "Wine of the worker."

"You are funny sometimes," she giggled, then climbed over him, rubbing the fabric of her panties against his cock, crushing it against his stomach.

He groaned as he adjusted himself underneath her, but she only rubbed harder against it.

"You really like me, don't you?" she whispered into his ear. "Like, more than you think you should, more than appropriate."

"If I say yes, will you stop crushing it?"

Serena shoved her tongue in his throat, perhaps as some sort of distraction to what she was doing under her dress. He tasted the coffee and her spit and groaned in good feeling as he felt her grasp his cock, pressing the tip against a silky wet opening.

Serena grunted, and then he felt her spread around

him, encompassing all his being as she slipped over and sheathed herself onto his swelling.

"Last night," she groaned, whispering into his ear, "I touched myself to the thought of you. Multiple times. I imagined it was your fingers touching me there, but I felt empty, so hollow, and needful for what you're giving me now."

Serena gritted her teeth, while Michael stared, full of euphoria as she thrust down onto him, pushing his cock deeper and deeper. Her soft, velvet walls teased every nerve ending he had, and some he didn't even know existed.

She began grinding back and forth. A wet feeling teased at the base of his balls and cock. He felt untold pleasure and feared he wouldn't last very long at all.

Her breasts squished under his grip. He nibbled on her nipple and gazed up at the goddess riding him, wondering what awful things she wanted him to do to her. He held but one idea from the search history he'd seen.

He could do that one.

As she increased her pace, her breath shortened, and sweet little moans escaped from her lips. "Oh..." she crooned, twisting and twirling her stomach like a wave. "Oh gods..."

Michael slid his fingers through her hair, pulled her closer, and bit down on the tip of her ear.

"Fuck!" she cried out. Her pussy blossomed like some

ballooning flower, soaking his cock in slickness, a sensual oil created for one purpose and one purpose alone, to bring out that which he tried with all his will to hold in.

She came, writhing and shaking, digging her nails painfully into his shoulders. "Unff!" Several noises came from her, like a wild animal that couldn't speak his language. "Unf, guh!" Several grunts and piercing cries followed.

And then she fell to him, while a balloon of pleasure swelled behind his navel, desperate for just one more thrust, and then it would be done.

She gazed into his eyes. Their crimson filled with euphoria, stroking his cheek. He felt like she felt things about him she hadn't even dared say. He knew she didn't just like him. She was suddenly obsessed with him to a dangerous level.

You shouldn't stick your dick in crazy, he thought, in his last grips of sanity. *And you definitely shouldn't come in them.*

But most of all, you shouldn't feel the same way as them. You should just run a mile and find someone less obsessed.

He would not run, and he'd already stuck his dick in her, but he could at least pull out. He wasn't *that* stupid.

Thankfully, he knew Serena possessed this crazed submissive streak that made him feel he could get away with his next sentence—nay, that she'd enjoy the words.

"Put it in your mouth."

She nodded enthusiastically and climbed off him, sliding off the couch like her body was coated in the most virgin olive oil. The dress stayed around her hips, the emerald green contrasting wonderfully with her lilac flesh. Her red lipstick had run everywhere, though, giving her this haunted Victorian look.

And as she pushed his legs apart, licked her lips, and dove around his swollen head, he thought it was the most glorious sight he'd ever seen.

Her tongue slithered around a glans surged with blood, lapping and licking around him. "Mmm," she said. "You taste so fucking good," she said when she popped his cock from her lips with a wet smacking sound.

"I think that's *you* you're tasting," Michael said.

"Then *I* taste so fucking good on you." She lapped her tongue around that hard, bone-like muscle on his underside, and he saw a bead of white drip out of the tip, then slip down the red flesh, leaving a trail amidst her spit, like a boat down a river.

Serena froze, catching sight of it, then a hunger flared in her eyes, and she shoved her mouth around his cock, pushing down to the middle as her tongue lashed against his tip, tasting the liquid.

"Guh!" She gagged as the tip of his cock pushed against her throat. She continued, though, gagging and gulping him down, making so much spit it poured down his balls and soaked her couch.

Michael gripped the couch, then her tits, then stroked her head, and kissed her upon the soft hair. His whole body tensed, filled with energy, ready to burst.

With a buck of his hips, submerging his cock down her throat, he grabbed her head to keep her steady while he throbbed release onto her tongue. Stars filled his eyes, and he let out an involuntary yelp.

Then, suddenly, that which was so engorged became tender, and each little tickle of her teeth felt like scraping blades.

He yelped again, and she gave that smile, that grin of mischief, gently resting her teeth against his glans.

He'd remember that sight until the day he died.

CHAPTER THIRTEEN

MICHAEL

Michael waited patiently for Serena to finish in the restroom. Thankfully, none of their 'passion' had dripped down to his jeans or boxers below, so it was a quick job of Serena wiping him up—with a crazed wildness in her eyes—and then scurrying away to tidy herself.

Eventually, her foot stomps carried her back to him.

"Is this appropriate?" she asked, barely looking him in the eyes.

Serena wore tight black jeans, her usual boots, and a baggy black sweater. In that outfit, she could have been mistaken for a burglar.

"I don't think they're going to care what you look

like," Michael replied. "They're just gonna be happy you're helping. Got a weapon?"

"*Weapon?*" she scowled. "Why would I need that?"

Michael shrugged. "You never know."

He knew why though. A faint inkling in the back of his mind knew why, and he dared not admit it, not to Serena and *especially* not to Wilson and Orla.

"Let's go," he said, walking toward the door, mind clear and guilt raging in him for not acting sooner. "I can't believe I convinced myself it was all fine, and we could just sit around doing nothing."

"You did all you could. You're not his parents," Serena said.

He turned and frowned at her. "Really?"

She darted her eyes away. "Come on then, let's go find the little prick."

"Nice," Michael said, rolling his eyes.

"What? I don't mean it. I don't even know him."

There she was. Serena, the one he really knew. He sighed and turned around. "Can you be a little more delicate when we get to their apartment? I just need to grab my stuff, and then we'll be out."

"That's not really one of my skills," Serena said, rubbing her arm and looking away. "Sorry, though." Her nose gave a little twitch. "It's not like I've pretended to be anything else than what I am!"

"Not including five minutes ago." Then, it hit Michael like a truck. "You feel bad. Is it guilt?"

"That's my secret, Michael, I always feel bad."

"Enough with the references. I hate those. It's just a cheap way to make jokes when you're not creative enough to come up with something yourself."

"Pah! You're a guy. You love all that nerdy stuff." She grinned at him.

"Haven't seen it," Michael said.

"You *haven't* seen it?"

"Nope."

"Then how'd you know what I was referencing?"

"Alright then!" Michael grabbed her hand and dragged her out the door, then swiftly brought her back so she could lock it.

In the night city streets of Stonereach, drunken women stumbled around them, arm in arm, as they sang some terrible song. Two men ate burgers, dropping salad on their shoes. Tourists snapped pictures of the glowing skyscrapers and billboards.

And walking through them were Serena and Michael, not close, but not far either, just walking beside each other, unsure of what had happened.

He wanted to grab her hand but felt she might tear it off. He wanted to ask her something but felt she might snap at him.

"You're a dickhead, you know that?" he said. *Oh my gods, I'm just like her.*

She just stopped, blinking at him and crossing her arms. He tried not to smile, knowing how to get under her skin. This was toxic. Very toxic. He didn't care one bit.

"Excuse me?" she said.

"One minute, you're all over me, telling me how much you like me, and the next, you're...this."

"This is what I've always been." Serena huffed like a petulant child.

"So you've told me."

"What are you gonna do about it?"

"You mean apart from taking you back home and spanking you?"

Her eyes rolled a little. "Don't," she said, a flicker of a smile forming.

He stepped closer, reached out, and fiddled with her ear.

Her pretty crimson eyes glazed over, and she bit her lip. "Ok, fine," she said, grabbing his collar and pulling him in with surprising strength to kiss him, making him push her up against the wall.

"PDA much," a woman complained, walking past.

"We have got to set you straight," Michael said, shaking his head at Serena.

"We?"

"Me."

She nodded, biting her lip again. "Maybe with some punishment." She cupped the back of his neck and pulled him in for another kiss.

"I've never been into all that BDSM stuff," Michael said.

"Neither am I," she replied. "Safe words, aftercare

—that's for hobbyists. I want to be *punished* in a way they would piss themselves at."

"I'm sure that would annoy them if they could hear you."

"Then they can take it up with me, not you." She stuck her tongue out. "I said it, not you, pretty Serena that no one can ever be mad at."

Michael nodded. "Anyway, this is a conversation for a later date," he said. "If I promise to...meet you halfway on that, will you meet me halfway on not being a dickhead?"

She huffed and nodded. "I promise to at least meet you halfway. I can't promise not to be moody. It's in my very soul." She then made the rockstar devil fingers and stuck her tongue out in some silly mockery of herself. Serena laughed in disbelief and then puckered her luxurious full lips out. They were without lipstick, a natural purple color now.

Michael liked it, and he kissed his moody, half-evil half-elf.

"Michael," she said.

"Yeah?"

"I meant everything I said. So...just remember that, please?"

"You mean remember that if you're being mean?"

She nodded.

"I can't ask you to be anything but yourself." He took her hand and dragged her toward his brother's place.

SERENA

Serena was awash with nerves.

Their elevator didn't even rock or creak. She didn't even feel like it was about to come crashing down were they to move a little. And before, when they entered the building, there was a woman at reception. Scratch that. They *had* a reception!

Serena squeezed Michael's hand, wishing she could apologize for her actions, but when he looked at her, she just gave him a little sneer.

She'd swallowed his cum. What did it matter how she treated him? He was inside her. He was *hers* now.

She winced. *No, it's not like that*, she thought. *She was his. His lovely little girlfriend with a cherry on top. Maybe she'd start wearing baby-blue sailor dresses and adopt a sunny disposition towards all the gods' creatures, great and small.*

She winced again.

"Stop wincing," Michael said. "What's wrong with you?"

"Have you got all night?"

Serena was too conflicted. Michael was going to have to tie her down to the bed, so she had no choice but to be submissive. She grinned, then looked at Michael, who was staring at her like she was crazy.

"I'm a little crazy," she explained.

"Yes, I can see that. Can you rein it in?"

"Can you rein *me* in?"

"Can anyone?"

"Perhaps only you."

The elevator continued to vibrate as it took her higher and higher.

"How do you know I can?" Michael said, crossing his arms.

"It's not that you can," Serena replied. "It's that you're the only person I've ever *wanted* to. Get it?"

"You're a very confusing individual, you know that, right?"

"Better than being a dickhead." She smirked.

"Maybe you're not. Maybe you're just troubled, and that's how it comes out."

"Wow, projecting much?"

"I am not troubled!" Michael cried a little too loudly.

"*I am not troubled!*" Serena repeated in a nerdy voice.

"I swear to the gods, when all this is over..." He rested a hand on the wall beside her head, leaning over her.

"Yes?" Serena bounced on her toes hopefully, twirling her hair and looking up at him all doe-eyed.

"I'm gonna have to do to you what was in your search history."

"Yes please." Her eyes glazed over.

"Then, be good?"

"I'll be a good girl." She pouted.

He rolled his eyes, then they kissed, the elevator dinged, and Michael took her hand, walking her down the hall. She trailed back a little, so he had to drag her like she was some obedient pet.

"You're very annoying, you know," Michael said.

Serena was beginning to sense that Michael thought that if he insulted her, she might get all wet and beg to be punished.

And if Michael thought that, then Michael was correct.

Or maybe he was just being honest.

"Two things can be true," she muttered.

"What's that?" Michael asked.

"Just remembering something a very wise, very smart writer once said."

They approached the door. Even the door looked fancy, with a golden frame around the number, and the door was painted a deep navy blue.

He put the key in, and in the hallway filled with loving family photos rushed a blonde, curly-haired woman and a man who looked sorta like Michael. They both had frantic worry on their faces.

A tidal wave of guilt washed over Serena. They'd been...canoodling, while his family was going through this?

She felt guilty for thinking the word *canoodling*, as well.

"Did you hear anything?" the man asked.

Wilson, Serena remembered. *His name is Wilson.*

"I'm gonna look around the usual haunts," Michael said. "Slayer bars. The guilds. You never know, he could be off his tits on drugs."

The woman squealed, covering her mouth in surprise. Then finally looked at Serena, rushed over, and extended her hand, taking Serena's with both of hers.

She smelled pretty.

"It's so nice to meet you," she said, sounding like she actually meant it too, despite the stress she was under.

"I thought Serena could help," Michael explained. "She's got some night-sight powers, and she's..."

Firstly, Serena wondered how he knew she could see better in the dark than a human, smiling a little at him knowing about her, then she wondered what he was going to say next before his voice trailed off.

But she did know.

"I'm strong," she said, bouncing on her feet. *Why do I keep doing that?* she wondered, *like some stupid manic pixie dream girl.* She crossed her arms and said, "Very strong. I can help."

Michael's shoulders tensed, and Serena frowned at that.

"W-what..." Orla began, worry washing over her. "What do you mean? Do you think he's in danger? But you said he wouldn't have been in that dungeon?"

Ah. Serena realized now why Michael didn't say it. Serena felt very stupid.

"Like I said," Michael began, "he's probably just out drunk somewhere. You know how kids can be. I'll find him."

"I'll grab my coat," Wilson said.

"No," Michael said. "You'll just slow me down. You stay here, look after Orla. She needs you."

Serena squinted, wondering if it would hurt Wilson's pride to be told that by his brother.

"He's...right. I can't lose two of you," Orla said, taking her husband's hand.

At that, Serena followed Michael down that hall of this offensively-nice-smelling apartment to a living room that looked straight out of a nineties sitcom about a suburban family.

Then they carried on to Tommy's bedroom, which smelled exactly as gross as a nineteen-year-old kid's bedroom would smell. They couldn't find anything, not even a laptop to try and crack the password of.

When they returned to the living room, Michael dug into some bags at the side of the couch, next to some rolled-up blankets and pillows.

This is where he sleeps? Serena thought. *He doesn't have a home. How sad.*

Serena wondered if she should invite him to stay at her place, then scowled, watching him put a gun around his hip.

"Fuck," she said.

"Hmm?" Michael asked as he got back up, checking his gear was all in order.

"Forgot my knife," Serena said.

"We've got knives!" Orla said, returning from the kitchen. "What's that, for cutting rope or something?"

"No, it's alright," Serena said, taking Orla's hand. "You are very, very pretty," Serena said.

Orla frowned. "Erm, thanks?"

"Come on," Michael said, grabbing Serena's hand in that forceful way she liked, pulling her out of the apartment. "I'll call if I find anything out!"

Once they were back in the elevator, Michael asked, "Why did you say that to Orla?"

"To distract her from what I'd just said, about my knife."

He nodded. "You did good," he said.

Serena bloomed some very odd feelings at those words, which confused her, and she wanted to insult him to bring her back to normalcy.

She didn't, she just bit her lip and mused on how screwed up she was inside.

CHAPTER
FOURTEEN

MICHAEL

Tents lined the fences, marked off with police tape. As Michael and Serena approached, he felt they were detectives working together on a case. *Not far from the truth.*

The night sky barely had a chance against the endless lights from phones and streetlamps. It wasn't natural to not be able to see the stars.

Oddly, he didn't yearn for it, like he thought he always would.

"There's no point," Serena said, pulling Michael out of his thoughts. "They won't let us in."

"I do have some sway," Michael replied, taking her hand and leading her along the tape line toward one of the bigger tents, which had more people going in and out than most.

"Sure, because you're a 'big cheese,'" Serena said dubiously.

They approached the tape to find a monkeykin woman with big fluffy ears poking out from under her police hat. Michael pulled out a badge from his belt and showed her.

"Is that real?" The policewoman frowned at it.

"Doesn't it *look* real?" Michael replied.

She squinted at him, and he felt Serena squint at him, too.

"Hang on," the monkeykin said, turning to interrupt one of her busy superiors. She pointed toward Michael, and they began whispering.

"You're a policeman?" Serena asked Michael.

"Where would I find time for that?" Michael replied.

Soon enough, the captain came over, checked Michael's badge, and shook his hand, introducing himself as Captain Vernon. "I thought you'd all gone extinct," he said.

"We tend to keep a low profile," Michael replied. "Easier that way."

"And..." Captain Vernon looked toward Serena.

"Miss Serena is my assistant," Michael said quickly. "She is highly qualified and as trustworthy as I am."

Michael lifted the tape and made an *after-you* gesture to Serena, who climbed under, and they followed the captain.

"You gonna explain that or what?" Serena asked, squinting at him.

"Have you really never searched my name on the internet?" Michael asked.

"Michael is a common name."

"My *last* name."

Serena blinked at him. "Erm..."

"You work with my uncle!"

"He just calls you Michael. And your last name is Walker, right?"

Michael nodded, glad his uncle wasn't loose-lipped. For all his supposed flaws, at least he had that going for him.

"It's no big deal," Michael explained as they followed Vernon into his tent.

"One minute you're a big cheese, the next, it's no big deal. *Uhhuh*, and I'm the indecisive one."

"You're *still* the indecisive one," Michael said. "And that's a polite word for it."

Soon enough, they stood at the captain's desk while the mustached man clicked his fingers to dismiss the policemen there so he could talk to Michael in privacy.

"We think a relic did it," Vernon said, spreading out some awful photographs of beheaded men with their jaws ripped clean open. One had eyes missing. "Rather, someone wielding it," he added.

"Or *it* wielding someone," Serena muttered.

As horrific as the situation was, Michael couldn't

help but look at the pretty drow with pride for her astute observation.

"Any idea who?" Michael asked.

"They were a tight-knit bunch of nogooders," the captain explained. "They always managed to avoid security cameras. We think it was from this one." He tapped the one Michael remembered as Brian. "Our mages found some vestigial mana lingering in him, an odd kind, unlike the usual. Something untethered about it. But then it was gone before they could run any tests. For some reason, they don't think it's related to their deaths. *Wizards*." Captain Vernon rolled his eyes.

Michael could agree with that sentiment. *Wizards*.

"So, you think there was a fourth member?" Michael asked. "The one wielding the relic? Any clue what the relic is?"

The captain pulled out another photograph of an ordinary street. Michael scowled, then looked closer. There was a shadow, an absence of light, snaking around like there was some error in the photograph.

He pulled out another, this time on another street corner beside a closed shoe shop. Once again, the absence of light, the shadow.

"We found this all the way from here," he explained. "It's the closest lead we've got. You ever seen something like this?"

"I take it you haven't," Michael replied. "Weren't

there some rumors of a queen's lost pearls down here? Augmented to let one see in the dark?"

"Understood just to be rumors," Vernon explained, scratching his chin. "Why such a specific augmentation, and one so simple at that? Artifacts with that augmentation aren't exactly rare. It's just some urban legend."

"Maybe a smoke screen," Michael said, looking at the shadowy, smokey figure in the photos. *Quite literally,* he thought.

"Does that badge of yours permit you to see the King?" Vernon asked.

"No more than yours does," Michael replied.

During this, Serena watched the two of them with a half-open mouth, clearly trying to hide her wonder at the situation. And in any other situation, Michael would've enjoyed that. He still did in this one, but if asked, he wouldn't admit it.

"Besides," Michael added, "no doubt the relic's origins are just as farcical as the abilities it was said to grant. Captain, the culprit may be Tommy Walker, a good kid of nineteen. Kind-hearted, if foolish enough to go digging into strange chests with some group of criminals. To do such things, he'd been manipulated or duped somehow and, at that, controlled via the mind to commit these atrocities. Will you go easy on him when you find him? He would not, ever, do what he's done willingly. He needs saving, not slaying."

Captain Vernon nodded. "We'll take that into

consideration." For a moment, his mouth opened slightly as if he wished to say something but thought better of it.

Michael had an idea of what it was. He was going to say that he would not spare Tommy's life if it meant they could save others. Tommy was a danger and had to be taken down.

"Hopefully, your wizards can do something," Michael said.

"They have no clue what it is," the captain said, apologizing with his eyes. Michael knew that meant they would be forced to fire destructive spells first and ask questions later.

"I've got some more stops to make," Michael said. "Can I get your number? I'll let you know if I discover anything."

"Good to have you on the team, Knightseeker."

They shook hands and exchanged numbers. Michael and Serena left the captain's tent to the inquisitive gazes of the policemen and women in the camp.

"You're joking," Serena finally said, as they strolled down the night streets. "He did not call you that."

Michael shrugged. "We're just a family." His modesty was very false.

"A family and an ancient guild of knights from the history books! Next thing you'll be telling me you're *Runeclaw*."

"That guy's real, too."

"Yeah, right."

"I *assume* he's real, anyway," Michael added. He tried not to show that he was enjoying this, then frowned.

"What is it?"

"Nothing," he lied. He was considering that he was just as screwed up as Serena was. His nephew was in danger, and he couldn't help but carry on like nothing had happened. Shouldn't he be full of worry?

No, that wouldn't help.

"We'll have to head back to the shop," Michael said. "See what illegal books ol' Patrick has that might shine a light on this. That's if you want to come."

Serena stared at him. "Of course I do. You'll need someone to read the words to you. *S* is the letter that looks like a snake."

"Acts like one, too," Michael replied.

"I do not!"

Serena grinned, looking away. Clearly, she was proud of his retort.

∼

SERENA

Serena held the badge in her hands, staring at it in disbelief. The words *Knightseeker* ran along the underside. There was a faint blue glow of a crest in the middle, apparently depicting its legitimacy. The crest was a knight on a hill, staring out into the distance.

"Thought you were a myth," Serena said.

"You think King's Knights are a myth," Michael retorted, dragging out a bunch of books from the safe under Patrick's desk.

"Never met one."

"Do you think the current king is a myth? You've never met him."

"Seen him on television, not the same."

"You're an elf! Your kind lives long enough to have met the King's Knights!"

"Dark elf, actually. My *kind* hardly canoodled with humans throughout history. We had our own thing going on."

"*Canoodled?*" Michael repeated. "Anyway, some of these grimores are completely unique. There might be something in here."

"Fine, let's split the pile and get studying."

Michael cocked his head at her.

"What?" she asked, feeling on the spot.

"Thanks for helping me," he said. "I appreciate it, especially when it has nothing to do with you. You could've just gone home and it would've been understandable."

"You help your friends," Serena said.

"*Friends*. Really?"

"Okay, fine, my oobi woobi boyfwend!" Serena was taking the piss, but she still blossomed with nerves at the words. She felt her cheeks go hot and turned away from him so he wouldn't see her blushing.

"*Friends* is fine for now, then," Michael said, chuckling.

Serena handed the badge back. "Does this mean I'm your squire?" she touched her lip. "Oh sire, no, don't gaze upon me with such hunger, tis quite inappropriate! I am but your student, innocent in the ways of adventure and love."

Michael ignored her, sitting at one of the chairs by the table at the other end of the room. He began pouring over the books, leaving Serena standing there staring at him.

"I best get to work then," she said.

∼

They spent forever pouring over books into the night. At about three a.m., the coffee was wearing off, as was their patience.

"Dunno why we'd expect to find anything," Serena said. "It's not like that wizard story where somehow the thirteen-year-olds go into the library to find information several veteran wizards couldn't, just by opening a few books that were freely available to be read by anyone."

"Funnily enough, that's how I find most of my jobs," Michael said, stretching and yawning. "And these books aren't freely available to read by anyone, forbidden part of the library or not. They're one-of-a-kind grimoires. Most people don't even know they exist."

"How did Patrick then?"

"He's a Knightseeker. Our network goes beyond the internet."

"Do you all wear funny pointy-hatted robes and conduct secret chanting rituals every Thursday, where you bend each other over in the name of the one true helmet?"

"That's Tuesday. On Thursday, we've got a quiz."

Serena snorted. "You are funny, sometimes."

"Keep saying that and you'll have to upgrade it to *all* the time." Michael yawned. "I'm exhausted and I've got nothing. Poor Wilson and Orla. This is why I'll never have kids."

"Never?" Serena asked, raised eyebrows.

"What good are kids when you're traveling like I am? Anyway, I can't seem to take these things seriously.'

"Maybe it's just being around me, making you put walls up against such things."

Michael sighed and gave a look of disdain. Serena thought he was getting tired of all these talks about feelings and backstory trauma.

"Believe it or not," he said, "I existed before you, and felt these things before you too."

They sat in silence for a moment, Serena picked at

her nails, and Michael slapped her hand away. "Stop that," he said.

She picked at them harder, pulling a hangnail. The pain seared like a lightning shock, and she cried out in pain.

"See?"

Serena pouted at him, closed her eyes, and felt herself drifting off, even with the pulsing pain in her finger.

She felt a nudge and opened her eyes.

"Not here," Michael said. "Come on, I'll take you home."

"How presumptuous," Serena said, holding her arms out so he could lift her up like a child.

She grinned as he did so—he was so strong!—but then let go so she was forced to walk.

"We'll work better when we sleep tomorrow," Serena said, yawning again.

They left the store, Michael locking up.

"We?" he questioned.

"If I'm not helping you, then I've got to work here, don't I?" She tapped her temple to indicate how smart she was.

"Very well," Michael said. "I would've liked to suggest we have a night apart, so we could have a second date proper, like a romantic gesture, or whatever."

Serena prodded his chest. "Incorrect," she said.

"You're going to hold me tonight so I can fall asleep in your big, strong arms."

He smiled. "Fair enough."

Then, she tiptoed up to his ear and whispered just what she wanted him to do to her.

And when they finally got home, they could barely get their clothes off before crashing into bed and falling asleep. Serena only got her jeans and shoes and one sock off, sleeping in her hoodie and thong, while Michael had his boxers and t-shirt. He grabbed her butt as he fell asleep, and Serena rubbed her groin against his thigh, falling asleep too.

CHAPTER
FIFTEEN

SERENA

Serena's eyes shot open. Birds were singing outside, the light crashing in, filtered through the sheets.

She felt a pressure on her, holding her down, like some warm weight was crushing her, in a good way. She felt...she felt invaded.

Michael split her open. The sweat between her legs was the only wetness to aid his morning wood crashing through her entrance. She cried out, trying to move, but he was grasping her wrists. Her feet flailed around, unable to do anything but bat against his thighs as he submerged into her, giving no heed to foreplay or making her wet enough.

"Like that?" Michael grunted, his morning breath turning her on.

Serena pushed herself up, feeling sore already, yet

wetness began to drip from her despite it already being too late.

She nodded, biting her lip so fiercely she feared she might rip through the flesh. "Like that," she gushed as he slammed down into her.

The bed creaked so loudly that it must have woken the neighbors. Michael became like some caveman, all urges and no care for her well-being.

"You're so...strong..." she muttered through gasping breaths, the pain giving way to a new pleasure, not just from how it felt to have him impaling her, nor from his groin crashing against her butt, making a dull slapping sound against the sheets as her cheeks compressed from his force, but from the very notion of him *claiming* her, making her his, with there nothing she could do about it.

Sure, she knew if she told him to stop, he would, but Serena would never do that. Why would she ruin something so wonderful?

He grunted and thrust into her, she tried to move her wrists up, but his strength kept her down. He was only a human. How was he so strong?

Then he bit down on her ear, she felt his teeth digging into the pointed ridges, and she bloomed arousal wetness. It dripped between her thighs, the sweat of his groin, his wet pubes. It all made such a mess before he'd even released any liquid.

Would he do it? Would he do it this time?

"Please," she murmured, scared to say it in case he

would say no. Scared to bring attention to it. He was scared of it as well. She knew it.

Michael stuffed her, his rageful cock so close to bursting she could *feel* it.

"Please," Serena cried again. "I need it."

She cursed herself. Now he knew what she meant.

Her eyes glazed over, her vision going blurry. Delicate ribbons inside her twirled around a ball of light. Every slam down into the bed was rubbing her clit against it. While he owned her from the inside, her outside was getting teased by his movement, too.

She dug her fingers into the bed and the pillow, nails nearly going through it. The light inside her grew greater, behind her navel first, then traveling down to her curling toes and up to the tips of her twitching ears.

Suddenly, her pussy swelled, engulfing his cock in warmth and desire. She felt it soak him and begged, begged with her last orgasming breath, begged him to come inside her.

"Guh!" she cried as his cock ripped out of her like they'd been one body, and all the wetness that splashed out was like blood from the wound.

He climbed over her, threw her over with force, and pushed the swollen glans inside her mouth. At the same time, she felt the lingering pleasure of her orgasm, slamming her hand against her clit to keep it going. In her mouth, he throbbed and released hot, tasty cum, coating her tongue, painting her throat in white oil as it slowly slid down like honey.

Michael crashed down beside her. His face was red, and his body was varnished in sweat. Serena lay beside him, resting her leg over him like one of his nameless courtesans, resting on her king before he would banish her until he was ready to lay again, that time with someone else. Of course, she would never allow such a thing, but the imagery of him being that powerful excited her. He certainly would have been in another time and place.

She swallowed, savoring the lingering taste on her lips as she looked at her warrior. He was panting from his efforts.

"My little purple princess," he said, kissing her forehead.

"Is that what you call this?" she replied, taking his cock with her finger and thumb and giving it a wiggle.

He winced, slapping her hand away. Serena giggled, thinking of all the evil ways she could torture him but would never dare.

"Let it be known," she said, resting her chin on his cheek and taking a long, deep scent of his sweat, "you may wake me up like that whenever we rest together."

"Noted." Michael nodded, then laughed, the aftereffects of paralysis broken. He sat up, pulled her up, and put his arm around her. She rested her fingers on his chest and threw her thigh over him again. "Food," she murmured, pushing off him to grab her phone.

"And back to work," he replied, grabbing for his own phone.

They browsed their phones silently for a while, neither getting food nor working.

"Oh, fuck," he said.

Serena frowned, ignoring Calra's message to gaze at Michael. The color had left his face, and his hands trembled. She frowned more, never having seen him be so affected by something.

Michael always took everything in his stride, *too* stridefull in fact. He never worried about anything, always doing what was right or what he thought was right, but never panicked himself into freezing up.

And now? His eyes were wide, and when he gazed at Serena, she thought it looked like a cry for help.

"What's wrong?" she asked, trying to still her own voice as she came back beside him to see what he was looking at on his phone.

There was an article. *Three Adventurers Dead Outside Guild*, it read.

"It could just be a coincidence," Serena said.

"Like the other party was a coincidence?" Michael rubbed his face.

"Is this a pattern?" she asked. "Does he have some reason to go after adventuring types?"

Michael scratched his chin. She could see him collecting himself, putting himself back together to meet the matter at hand.

And she felt...oddly proud of him. *What a man he is.*

"That's who's let him down," Michael said. "First me, then that awful group that took him there in the first place."

"But you're not an adventurer. You're a tomb raider."

"Same same, and I doubt that evil controlling him cares to split hairs. It's just using his emotions against him."

He got up from the bed. Serena resisted the urge to lunge for his muscular thigh and gnaw on it. She didn't even know why she wanted to.

∼

MICHAEL

"I spoke to the police captain when you were in the shower," Michael said. "Explained to him my suspicions. Hopefully, their wizards can use that information to find a spell to undo it." He and Serena paced down the street, coffees in hand. Michael was glad he'd had the forethought to bring a spare change of clothes. "Do you remember any sort of creature like that in the books we read?" he asked.

"No, but...Michael, what if they consider that as a reason for his guilt?"

"Better him in jail than others dying because of it," he said, feeling stone-faced and heartless. He meant it.

They could get him out of jail eventually. They could never bring back those lives.

They were walking in the direction of the store to see if they could find anything in those books again. Now, they had more of a concrete idea to look for.

Serena wore her boots as usual and a long black dress that turned to maroon in a gradient at the bottom, flowing around her ankles. He cursed himself for even caring about what she was wearing at a time like this, yet it calmed him a little, he supposed.

"You look nice," he said.

"Thanks," she replied, looking away and smiling. Then she took his arm and tiptoed up to kiss him on the cheek.

"What's made you so sweet all of a sudden?"

"Do you not like it?"

"No, I lo—it's great," he said, quickly changing what he was about to say. *Phew, that was close.*

"I suppose it's what you did to me this morning." She grinned. "Do it again?"

Serena quickly looked around, and then gave his groin a little stroke.

He grabbed her wrist. "Obviously not here," he said, slotting his fingers into her hand again.

They continued their journey down the street, finding the shop door lights on.

"Fuck sake," he said. "We forgot to turn the lights off." Michael pulled his key out and slotted it, turning to find it was already unlocked.

Widening his eyes, he pushed the door open to find customers already browsing the shop.

He rushed through the shelf and found an older man he knew, with lines of tiredness in his red eyes, but otherwise healthy, on his feet at the counter.

"Patrick!" he said, rushing forward to greet him. "Why didn't you get the hospital to call me?"

Patrick looked up. "Ello kiddo. You left my place in a mess." He had a warm smile, if a little weak.

His polo t-shirt was a little disheveled, the top two buttons undone, revealing blue lightning lines of toxin running up his neck.

"Don't they have rules about not discharging people alone?" Michael asked in disbelief.

"Bah, I walked out. What were they gonna do, arrest me?"

Michael shook his head. "Patrick, did you hear about Tommy?"

Michael quickly filled him in on the news, and during the story, he frowned and turned around, realizing Serena wasn't with him.

"That explains the books," Patrick said. "Come on, there's something familiar there. Lemme have a look in my books."

"Hang on, I'll just grab Serena."

Patrick looked above him and indicated to the mirror that reflected to the door. Serena was standing by the door still, just inside, hesitant to come forth.

"You talk to the police?" Michael asked. "About your situation, I mean."

"Not yet," Patrick replied, a flicker of a smile in his ragged mouth.

"Patrick," Michael warned. "You will tell them she didn't try to kill you, right?"

"Didn't she?" He raised his eyebrows. "How do you know?"

"Because she wouldn't—" Michael hesitated. Could he be so blinded by...lust, that he would fall for her lies? "Patrick. I'm your nephew, be honest."

"And Tommy's *your* nephew, so let's get to finding him."

"Fine. I'll just go and get Serena."

"Tell her she's fired, wouldn't you?"

"Patrick, I don't wish to hit an old man, especially one that's just gotten out of the hospital, but you sure make it tempting. Stop it now. She's been helping me find Tommy, and we could still use her help."

"Helping? She couldn't even help out here. No, we'll do fine on our own."

"Yeah, nah, you can get fucked. She's helping."

Michael stormed around the corner of the shop, coming back to grab Serena, not knowing just what would even happen. How would they work together? How could he make Patrick see he was an asshole, and Michael convince himself that she didn't do what he claimed? It seemed more plausible she could by the second. She was batshit, he knew that full well.

He got to the front door. There was nobody there but a customer.

"Did you see a pretty drow here?" Michael asked.

The man shook his head, continuing to peer over the goods in the display, so Michael ran out to the street, only finding shoppers and families. He ran around the corner of the turning, hoping she'd taken a swift left, but he couldn't see her, so he pulled out his phone and rang her.

She did not pick up.

CHAPTER
SIXTEEN

MICHAEL

Michael touched his Knightseeker badge in contemplation.

The walk back to the shop felt wrong, yet the correct thing to do.

They'd been ripped apart from each other; rather, Serena had ripped herself away, and Michael could hardly blame her. She bore some trauma about Patrick they'd hardly addressed, patching over it with a useless bandage.

In any other situation, Michael might have gone after her—like his silly name suggested, *seeking the night elf.*

A few hurt feelings could be mended later. People's lives were at stake. And if they truly were meant to be together, a simple day or two apart would not change that. He had to trust Serena felt the same.

Michael approached the door, remembering all the times he walked in to greet her. *Yeah, all both of them.*

"Ya done fucking about?" Patrick asked. "Or are we gonna save Tommy?"

Crass as Patrick was, Michael couldn't deny he *had* been fucking about, downplaying and denying the danger so he could have just one more crumb of drow pussy.

He tried not to snort. She would've found that funny—and agreed with it too.

"I'm surprised there's something in those books we missed," Michael said.

"I'm not," Patrick replied. "Come on." He indicated for him to follow, then the beads caught in his face and he got tangled in them like vines. "Bastard things, who put these down! Bet it was that *drow*."

Michael didn't like how he said drow—overpronounced with venom. Like the word was a swear itself.

Michael's fingers twitched. "No insulting Serena around me," he said simply.

"Oh? A little cunt-struck, are we?"

Michael closed his eyes for a moment. Patrick was always horribly perceptive.

"Better than being a bitter old asshole struck by his own self-importance," Michael said. "Do you jack off to porn, or just gaze at your wrinkly old todger in the mirror?"

Patrick chuckled as he led Michael toward the back room. "You can only count on yourself," Patrick said.

"Maybe," Michael replied. "Maybe not. You count on *me*, don't you? I don't see you running into those tombs."

"That's because you're like me, my boy. All we need is each other."

"Fair," Michael said, swallowing as he tried to still his feelings. "Maybe I just need time to get back to how we used to," he said. "All this city life got into me like a toxin. I feel it shaking off already."

"Aye," Patrick said.

Patrick could see where he was going. *Be more subtle,* Michael told himself.

"Could've tidied up the place," Patrick said as they entered his office to find the books sprawled all over the desk and floor.

"We were a little preoccupied," Michael replied coolly.

The old bloke traveled toward the wall behind his desk, where he peered up at the poster, gave Michael a stern look, and pulled at the left pin holding it up, then one in the middle of Amerthorn. His hand traveled across the great sea to their realm of Greenhaven and the city of Stonereach, and he pulled that pin.

The wall gave a click, and Michael's eyebrows raised. "A trick door," he said. "Surprised I never figured that out."

"An old man's got to keep a few tricks up his

sleeve," Patrick replied, pushing the door open to blackness until he fumbled around with his arm inside. Some lamps lit up, illuminating the room's shiny contents.

Michael followed him inside and gasped. There it was—the knightseeker uniform. A short blue and red cape, the leather armor a darker blue and red, mostly brown unless you looked at it more closely. The steel shoulder, elbow, and knee armor were dull with dust, and the blade behind it in the glass cabinet of items looked like it hadn't been drawn in centuries. Neither had all the fancy tools and weapons, ancient and useless now. Michael looked away from them. *Just relics now,* he thought. *Hidden in his tomb for nobody to find.*

Michael touched the shoulder pommels, then the shining badge of self-importance on the chest.

"Thought these had all been lost," he said. "Why'd you keep this from me?"

"Same reason it was kept from me until I was too old to wear it. We don't want the youth to get funny ideas. There's no money in saving people."

"We best leave Tommy to his own devices then."

"Very funny." Patrick hobbled over to a bookshelf in the corner, where a very particular chest rested above the top of it.

Michael walked over and peered at the mimic.

"Don't touch her!" Patrick cried.

He hobbled over and nudged Michael out of the

way. Suddenly, a purple tongue slipped out of the gap of the lid. Eyes snapped open atop it, the two parts of wood spreading apart like flesh. A giant purple, slivering wet tongue quested for Patrick like it wanted to eat him.

"Soon, baby, soon," Patrick said, stroking the wood tenderly.

Michael felt faint and wished to know absolutely nothing of what 'soon' meant, though he feared he knew exactly what. Sod 'secrecy of their lineage,' Patrick wanted to keep this room secret for *that*.

Michael felt more queasy and decided to change the subject to a much more important one. "Why do you hate drow?" Michael asked as Patrick thrust open the book before him.

"I don't," Patrick said. "I hate *that* drow. Thinks she's better than everyone. Pretended to be polite on the first day, then acted like she owned the place moments later. Big tits don't make you a big cheese."

Something about milk, Michael thought in the back of his mind. "That will be the last time you mention her tits again," he said.

Patrick waved away his words, and Michael shoved his shoulder—gently, but enough to show he wasn't messing around.

"Fine, have it your way," Patrick said.

"So why all the drow hate?" Michael asked. "If you don't hate them."

"Because it hurts her," he said absentmindedly, thumbing through the book on the table.

"Fine, you prick. Tell me this—did she try to kill you?"

Patrick sighed. "If I wanted to fuck with her about that, I'd be putting myself under scrutiny, wouldn't I? She knows that I know that."

Michael squinted at the bushy-eyebrowed prick and said, "What would that matter? You already flaunt the Emerald Knight's sword out your window."

"Well, that's a fake innit. Just for decoration." Patrick grinned knowingly.

"Hidden in plain sight. You're a funny guy, you know that?"

"It doesn't matter what you've got. It's how you got it."

"And you've grown arrogant. The younger you would never do such a thing."

Patrick grinned. "They don't know, I could be some long-lost relative of ol' Sir Elliot Reed. Half the realm doesn't even think they existed, and any nobles walking past will just assume it's a fake. There's plenty of those knocking about."

"Whatever, I'm just glad you admitted Serena didn't try to kill you. Now, shall we get on with it?"

"Didn't I?" Patrick grinned. "I said I couldn't *claim* she did it. I never said she didn't."

"Oh fuck you, you bastard." Michael stared at his

uncle in disbelief and said, "Show me how to save Tommy so I can be rid of the sight of you."

∼

SERENA

Calra wasn't responding to Serena's messages, no doubt hungover, in the arms of Clint, after getting dicked down to her heart's content.

"This is what I get for only having one friend," Serena muttered. "Still, one more than Michael." She thought she'd chuckle at that, but the comment stabbed at her like a little red dagger with a heart pommel.

"Eww," she said. "What a gross thing to think. That sounds like something *he'd* say. Anyway."

Serena grabbed the controller on her couch, and turned on the television, eager to finally get back into the game she'd been neglecting. She played every evening, and the break had been too long. She'd probably forgotten where she was or what the buttons even did.

I should be helping Michael, Serena thought. Whereas a dagger had stabbed her before, that was more like a sword. *No, don't be stupid. He does this kind of thing for a living. He doesn't need you getting in the way.*

Besides, he made his choice. Patrick over her. They were blood.

Serena shook her head. She was being dramatic. A day apart wasn't going to kill them. That's what normal people do when they date. They go on a date, and then spend a week apart and then go on another date and on and on, and then hopefully, one of them blows their brains out to end all the constant *'Am I staying at your place tonight, or mine?'* or *'I don't want to watch that movie, it sucks, let's watch this one.'*

Serena felt a little pain in her chest. She'd very much like to watch a movie she hated with Michael right now. She would pretend to like it even if she didn't, just to see the dumb, pleased look on his face when she was doing something that made him happy, and then eventually, she'd even like the movie, and it'd become something they'd bond over and show their ki—

She broke herself off from that thought. *Nope, don't think that. He's made it very clear how he feels about that topic. And anyway, we only had one date. Don't get crazy.*

She should text him.

Nope.

She should.

Nope.

If only Calra and Clint were there to tell her what to do.

Serena shook her head and shivered. She grabbed her laptop, opened the search bar, and typed *A*.

There it was. She trembled in anticipation. Every time she tried on herself, it was...a lot, too much, even. But if *he* did it? She'd be utterly destroyed from the inside out.

That'd be awesome.

A warmth blossomed through her nethers, and she put her legs on the couch to lay on it, stroking over the rough fabric of her jeans. A trembling, fiery pleasure broke through the confines of her clothing.

What if...what if she wore it the next time he came over? Then he could pull it out, and it might make a *pop* sound like a lollipop.

Serena convulsed in desire, her back arching up as she grasped between her legs. There was more to the feeling now. She wasn't just touching herself—in fact, she was hardly doing it at all, and yet the overwhelming swelling of need within her made her eyes go euphoric with feral desire.

He'll never trust you, though, her inner thought said. *He'll always wonder if you did it.*

"Shut up, shut up, shut up!" Serena slapped the side of her head, remembering all those times she used to smack her head and thigh, trying to keep herself sane.

She knew only one way.

She threw her legs off the couch, ran to her bedroom where the red lamp was already lit, then fell over and smacked into the bed, face first.

Serena smelt their sex, their sweat, their bodies.

She grabbed the sheets and shoved her nose so deep into them it smushed it. She shivered in need as she sniffed it.

If Michael decided to hate her and leave her, she may never wash the sheets again.

He wouldn't do that, she told herself. *He's as obsessed with you as you are with him.*

I should text him.

"No!" she yelled and dug out the bedside cabinet, the precious metal bulb with the spiky heart base. She'd had it custom-designed on the internet, explaining she wanted the spikes to be just at the edge of safety for a drow, not a human.

She did not mention she was half-drow. That would be somewhere in the middle—far too safe for her needs.

As she traced her fingers across the spiky edges, feeling the delectable sharpness, she trembled in nervous excitement.

Putting it by the pillow, she grabbed the lubricant, poured a small gloop onto her finger, and then cursed her stupidity because she hadn't even taken her jeans off. No matter. She pulled them down to the top of her thighs, then her thong which peeled out from between her fat cheeks. She poured another little bit of the white slimy liquid again, then spread her cheeks and touched her forbidden hole, shivering in trembling desire.

Nerve endings cried out in surprise at the cold

liquid, soon becoming warm as she rubbed it in, tracing circles, resisting the urge to touch her clit with her other hand. That would be left to cry out for attention, but it didn't deserve it.

Serena deserved some good old-fashioned pain.

The tip of her finger pushed into her forbidden entrance, spreading the tight, grasping star of flesh apart to invade herself. Her legs shook, and her hole protested with a dull pain, but the slickness of her finger could not be stopped. She pushed through herself and cried out, the beginning of some tears forming, wetting her pillow.

Serena slid a curled finger in and out of herself, her hole squeezing tighter in protest, not loosening one bit.

Drow was not supposed to admit the most taboo-to-mention stereotype about them was completely true. Drow loved anal more than any other race in the realm combined. Some humans liked it; all drow *loved* it.

"Call me a dirty little drow," she murmured, picturing it wasn't her finger but *his*. "Tell me this is all I'm good for."

She slipped her finger out, worried if she continued she'd get too used to it, and the feeling would be less intense, that the bulb would slip in with no protest. It shouldn't be easy. It should hurt.

Yet she knew that there would be no amount of preparation that would get used to Michael's thick, girthy length invading her there. She could try and try, and no matter what, he would split her open.

She hoped he wouldn't go too easy on her.

She should text him.

"No!" Serena cried as she grabbed the bulb, clasping her hand around the spiky outside to let it dig into her flesh. Then she pushed—without any further coating of lubricant—the bulb into her anus.

"Guh." Serena let out a grunt, then lots of whimpering whines. She gritted her teeth and felt more tears of pleasure slip from her eyes. Her legs shook and trembled like a newborn deer's. As the tip pushed through, her hole swallowed the metal, sucking it in with a force that shook her whole body, both in pain and ecstasy.

The spikey base pressed against her buttcheeks. She let go, and the cheeks hugged further into the points, making her cry out at the perfect crossroad between pleasure and pain.

"Gah!" she cried, gripping the covers and pillows and wincing. "You can do it!" she urged herself. "Be a good girl and take your punishment."

Instead of pushing herself to her knees, as she had done when she'd tried this before, then spreading her legs to lessen the punishment, she clenched her buttocks, pushing either cheek against the edges, making them dig deep into the flesh, securing the base in place, so that she and the bulb were truly one.

"Fuck!"

Serena dug her fingers into her jeans and rammed them against her swollen budding clit like she wanted to hurt it, roughly rubbing it until she soaked her jeans with an overflowing orgasm. Her eyes swelled up with euphoria. The light traveled through her whole body, starting and ending at her clit and forbidden hole. The more she spasmed, the more her buttocks swelled around the spiky base.

"Yes! Oh fuck oh fuck! Unf."

The orgasm continued well past what should have been normal, endless trembling pleasure shooting through her, soaking her jeans further as she pinched a nipple so tight it stung with pain.

Finally, she turned on her back and spread and bent her legs like Michael was pushing back on them to fuck her. She was alleviating the pain now, the spikes just tickling against her cheeks. It wasn't like they were sharp enough to actually cut her, just to administer her much-needed punishment, reward. Punishing reward.

Then, she grabbed her phone. She could text him now, as a treat.

Just one text. Not two. That would be stalkerish.

CHAPTER
SEVENTEEN

MICHAEL

"What's that?" Captain Vernon said over the phone as Michael paced the streets. His gun was hidden firmly under his shirt.

"It's not him," Michael said. "It's a copy. From a soulstealer mimic. Do you still have the mimic locked away?"

"Mimic? It was an empty chest. It's just sitting there."

Michael rubbed his face. "Go secure it. *Don't* touch it! If we don't get the soul back to Tommy first, he'll die."

"Knightseeker," the captain said with trepidation. "*Michael*, you know what we'll have to do if it comes to it."

Michael's phone vibrated.

"Where was it last seen?" Michael asked, gripping the page in his hand, worried he'd damage it but scared to let it go. He had to read from the words in time to docile the spirit, all while it would be trying to kill him.

His phone vibrated again.

"It's killed again," Captain Vernon said. "We managed to keep this one under wraps. A pair of adventures, man and wife. If the news found out about this one, it'd be all over. The city would riot with panic."

And all over for Tommy, Michael thought. It didn't matter if it was him or not. If they caught it and it had his appearance, no amount of supernatural explanation would calm the panicked mob looking for a villain to blame.

"I appreciate you bringing me in on this," Michael said. "Not normal for a police captain to trust a civilian with sensitive info. I hope you don't get in trouble."

"Civilian? Are you kidding? You're a Knightseeker! Once upon a time, we were taking orders from you. History may have forgotten, but we don't. You save the kid, and I bet you'll get a real knighthood from this, and your status will be recognized by all."

"I'm more than happy with the anonymity," Michael replied as his phone vibrated for a third time. "Send me the address of the last crime scene, please."

They ended the call, and Michael's phone vibrated *again*.

"What!" Michael yelled, opening his messages.

Hey, Serena had texted.

You mad at me? she texted.

Sorry, she texted.

Oh my gods you're mad at me.

Well screw you anyway!

The texts flooded in, one another the other. A scroll bar appeared on the screen, its controller shrinking to a smaller and smaller rectangle.

I'll never leave your side again.

You want that, right?

I want that.

I know you want it.

You better want it.

It's just you and me, Michael. You and me against the world.

The world is our enemy, Michael. We're the only ones we've got. It's just Serena and Michael FOREVER AND EVER! A hundred years, Serena and Michael!

Do you get that reference? It's from a show you probably haven't seen.

To be fair, you have to have a high IQ to understand it.

That's another reference, from a meme about it.

Do you know what a meme is?

Of course you don't.

That's okay. I can look past it.

Just like you can look past my flaws, right?
You can fix me, right?
My butt hurts.
Don't ask!
Okay, I'll tell you.

"Good lords," Michael said in disbelief. **I'll text you later**, he replied. Then he swiftly checked the address Captain Vernon had sent him and put his phone in his pocket as it vibrated away.

He scowled, wishing he could just turn it off. Instead, he dug into his settings and found a way to make any notification from Serena silent.

"Sorry, babe," he said aloud. "You're batshit, but not in a murderous way. I'll deal with you when all this is over."

∼

Michael inched his gaze to the corner of the brick wall, peering through the chain-link fence that had been ripped clean open. An odd, smokey, blood-like substance clung to the tears in the chains.

It can bleed, at least, Michael thought.

How had he never encountered something like this before? He supposed it was a city-specific monster, once a normal mimic infected by the poison of industry.

Wax lyrical later, he urged himself, then gingerly crept through the fence gap, and paced up to where the massacre had taken place. He figured that while the monster was mad at adventurers and the like, it'd be mad at Michael above all for kickstarting the whole thing.

There were no dead bodies. The police had cleaned it up as discreetly as they could, though some odd stains appeared on the ground, like puddles of oil.

Michael looked around, spotting a hole in the wall. Perhaps a magic bolt had fired there as the adventurers fought back.

Michael grabbed the scroll in his hand, shakily waiting for something to appear, considering it a fool's errand. He sniffed, the scent of car congestion and dirt pilfered his nostrils. He expected to be snorting black when he went back home.

He sighed, going to pocket the scroll, when a gust of wind like a thunderbolt slammed past him, knocking him off his feet in a twirl of death.

Michael continued the spin to plant his feet steady again. The creature had paused, the faint outlines of arms and legs visible in the smoky apparition. He undid the scroll with deathly steady hands, his periphery keeping an eye on the creature while he quickly murmured the words, "*Ree, laa na —*"

The ghostly apparition slammed right into him, tearing through the paper. A black ink infected the page, burning it like cinder flames.

As Michael fell to the ground, he subtly reached for

his gun, cocked it, and the moment he hit the ground, fired a shot at the thing's leg.

Just like Michael had been hit with an arrow way in the tomb, so had Tommy's mimic.

The creature fell to its knee, the ghostly pale form morphing right into Tommy's face, his youthful features crying in anger, as the pale black blood spilled from the wound in his knee.

"You hurt me!" it said, half sounding like Tommy, half a haunted, gurgling sound like its tongue was too big. "You! You did this!"

"I'm just trying to help you," Michael said, pushing himself up.

"Me? Me? *You* help me? Then why did you push me away? Couldn't help me down there, could you? *Uncle Michael.*"

Michael had to get this right. If he wanted to shoot again, he had to cock the gun quickly. One wrong move, and it'd lunge for him.

It had destroyed the scroll. Now, all that was left was Michael.

"I was trying to help both of you, actually," Michael said. "You and the mimic. Get you both back where you belong."

That's it. Keep it talking.

"Me..." the mimic said. "Heh. I get it now."

A sudden jolt of fear snaked up Michael's spine.

The mimic took a step toward him. And then swiftly dissipated into a ghostly apparition once more, though the head of Tommy remained at the top of the ghost. It flew through the gate Michael had climbed in.

Michael cocked the hammer, aiming for another extremity, but some civilians walked past, and Michael pulled the gun back.

The mimic spirit was gone, and Michael knew just where it was going.

His mouth was dry. He had to act fast.

He'd told Captain Vernon to secure the chest. The place would be swarming with wizards and police.

Shit.

∽

SERENA

She stared at her phone in disbelief. Sitting cross-legged on her bed with her jeans now pulled up, the big damp patch was like a wet halo for her phone to rest on. Praise the gods they made them waterproof now, though her case was enough to protect it.

Her butt ached, the buttplug pushed diagonally against her hole as the bed forced up against it.

That was the least of her problems, though. When her manic tirade had finally subsided, she bore witness to...a hundred messages left for him.

Ten would've been too much. Five would've been cause for alarm. Three would raise an eyebrow, but...a hundred?

Granted, at one point, she started going into her lore theories about Elven Ring, so at least he would've found that exceedingly interesting. She was certain of that. Everyone found Elven Ring lore interesting, even if they'd never played it.

Or maybe Calra was just being nice when she listened to her talk about it.

Speaking of, her phone started ringing.

"Hey!" Serena said, both meekly and frightened.

"What's up, babe?" Calra replied down the phone. "I got your message. Is something wrong?"

"Erm, nothing. I just sent Michael a hundred messages."

"Right..."

"Yeah."

"Well, there's plenty more fish in the sea."

Serena threw her head against the pillow, bending her legs in the fetal position, feeling her anus clench the bulb, shivering as she felt her insides invaded by the cool metal jewelry. It wasn't a sex toy, it was more like a necklace she'd wear forever and ever and ever.

"What if he just thinks I'm quirky?" Serena asked. "Like a Chloe De'flannel character?"

"Do you want support, or advice?" Calra asked.

"I want you to give it to me straight," Serena said, without a second of hesitation. She clenched her fist and bit it, while she clenched her butt to more strongly feel the bulb.

"Well, babe, if you texted him *literally* a hundred

times, and then he's the kinda guy to be totally cool with that, I'm not sure he's someone I want you with."

Serena nodded, a tear sliding down her cheek. She felt all empty again, hollow, this time with no hope of Michael filling her. Even the plug inside her was just a stopgap. The moment she pulled it out, she'd deflate and become nothing.

"I thought he could fix me," Serena said.

"Not sure anyone can do that, babe, and I'd rather you didn't make each other worse."

Serena bit her lip. "And if I ignore you and find him and make him love me no matter what?"

"As long as you're not *too* insane, I'll still support you. Just because I think it's a bad idea doesn't mean I can't be proven wrong. My parents hated the idea of a troll, but now they love Clint! And I haven't even met Michael, so...yeah. Fuck, I think I may have given you the wrong advice. Keep your distance, Serena! Let it settle first!"

Serena grinned. "I won't be keeping my distance, I'll be closer to him than he can even imagine."

"Okay, erm, just try and be normal about it?"

"I'll be totally normal, don't worry!" Serena climbed off the bed, resisting a moan that'd alert Calra to the bulbous object prodding her rectum. She reached under her bed, pulling out the sacred chest gifted to her by her mother.

She unclasped the ties and pushed open the purple

and black box, and the knife gleamed a purply hue at her.

My knife, she thought with delight. *Yes. This is what I need.*

Serena grinned, biting her lip and drawing blood.

CHAPTER
EIGHTEEN

MICHAEL

"You need to find a way to force the apparition back into the chest," Patrick explained over the car speaker. "Once you do that, Tommy's body should appear, and you can yank it out."

"And if the mimic gets to its chest first?" Michael asked.

"One second. I had a note here." Pages flicked back and forth over the speakers. "Ah, yes. On rare occasions, soulstealer mimics have been known to possess a tendency to try and destroy the host body, thinking they can go on without their chest. Michael. You can't kill it. I'm sure you've already figured that out by now. Tommy's soul will be lost to the ether."

Michael was already zooming down the highway, and he pushed the pedal further. He really didn't want to get pulled over and have to explain the situation. The police at the crime scene had understood his badge's importance. Who's to say this one would? Yet he was close. So close.

Soon enough, he parked his car and paced toward the crime scene, spotting wizards in guard posts dotted along the alleyways and sidewalks. The monkeykin policewoman then let him underneath the tape.

At the entrance to the sewer door, several wizards in colorful sweaters and pointy armored hats stood around, keeping beady eyes on their surroundings. Their staffs fizzled with magic energy, blue sparks spitting from the orb at the tip of one, green on the other.

Michael was let into the captain's tent. Captain Vernon paused for a moment in apprehension, then relaxed his shoulders upon seeing it was him.

There was a wizard there, too, a gray-bearded fellow who introduced himself as Alabaster. He wore a strange mix of police and wizard attire: a bulletproof vest draped in stars and a wizard's hat with a black and white checkered band running around it.

Michael explained the situation as best as he could.

The captain scratched his chin. "So you need to keep the chest from it *and* put it inside it? How exactly do you expect us to do both?"

"Can't you run some illusion?" Michael asked Alabaster.

"Upon a general mortal, yes," Alabaster replied, "but this creature is new to us. It operates on a different ethereal frequency to any creature to whom we've attuned our spells. This is why we've been unable to reveal the illusion that hides Tommy in the chest. But if we held that grimoire..." Alabaster turned to Captain Vernon and spat, "Tell me, why has it been kept from us?"

"Well?" Captain Vernon said to Michael.

Michael dared not throw his uncle under the bus, lest he throw himself in there, too, and perhaps even Serena. "There's no law against keeping grimoires to yourself," he said. "How was my source to know they held the only copy?"

"Perhaps via their manner of obtaining it?" Alabaster said, stroking his long silver beard.

Wizards, Michael groaned internally. "Maybe we can deal with that after," he said. "Let's focus on saving my nephew." A sudden idea flared inside Michael. "I'll make you both a deal."

"Oh, he makes deals now," Alabaster said with a roll of the eyes.

"Yes, *he* does," Michael replied. "Captain Vernon, I'll gracefully accept my knighthood if it's offered, and speak proudly of how you aided me, the first true Knightseeker in generations."

Captain Vernon lit up at that, then swiftly tried to hide it. "Yes, and?"

"Alabaster, I will speak to my source and get him to release his top-secret grimoires to the police so that this knowledge can be used to save countless lives in the future. Oh, and it will give you plenty of nighttime reading."

The wizard started drooling at the thought of some new grimoires to ponder over. "Well, I shan't say no to—"

"Michael," Captain Vernon interrupted. "What's to stop me from arresting you and finding your source by force? I'm sure it wouldn't be hard to find. Who's to say I haven't already?"

Michael shrugged. "Never knew a man in power who held no ambition for it. Maybe they could make you a constable, or even a lord. Sure, they'll give you a little promotion for scraping what grimoires and secrets you can before my source's safety measures are enacted to keep them out of your hands, but do you really think those morsels would be as favorable to the King as aiding the Knightseeker in saving the city and the endless wealth of knowledge available to you?"

They both stood in contemplation for a moment, giving each other looks that Michael worried portrayed a secret message he was unaware of.

"So it's *the* Knightseeker now, is it?" Captain Vernon said with a grin.

"I see no others in this tent."

Suddenly, a commotion rang out behind them. There was the distinct sound of magic spells being spoken and the thunderous humming sound of their magic connecting with their target.

Michael ran out of the tent to the gloomy afternoon, toward the tape. Just outside it, a lilac-skinned elf lay on all fours on the pavement, shackles of light on her wrists and ankles, holding her down.

She arched her neck up, her glasses fell to the ground before her, and her crimson eyes stared into Michael's soul, lighting some terrifying feelings in him.

"Erm..." Michael said, then noticed the glowing purple knife that'd dropped from her hand. The blade bore serrated edges and a dark purple line, making up the blade edge of the blade. The leather was an ebony so dark it sucked in the light around it.

"What's the meaning of this?" Michael yelled, making a few of the wizards jump. The shackles fizzled slightly.

"She was demanding entry," one said. "We sensed the drow weapon on her, and she pulled it out, claiming it was just a precaution."

"Captain," Michael said cooly to Captain Vernon. "Please order your men to release my partner. It's long been appropriate for a Knightseeker to carry a weapon in the city."

The captain squinted, clearly thinking that while

Michael was a Knightseeker, she was clearly not. Still, he nodded to the wizards.

The lights dissipated from Serena's wrists and arms, and she pushed herself up. She picked up her dagger and slotted it in the scabbard at the back of her belt, then dusted herself off as if nothing had happened—rather, it seemed, trying to give off that impression.

"That's one way to make an entrance," Michael said, cooling his voice so the police would believe nothing was wrong.

Serena's eyes were shot wide, her pupils pinpricks as they looked into his soul.

A flash of warning shot up Michael's spine. Something was wrong with her. It was like she was... vibrating with energy. *As if her texts hadn't been warning enough.*

Michael walked toward her and said, "Come, we've got important business to discuss on the situation. Captain, can we take a tent?"

The captain nodded, looking dubiously at Michael.

"Assuming the chest is kept safe," Michael asked, "will there be any warning if the mimic gets close?"

"Several wizards posted along the way," Vernon replied. "No need for you to stand watch too." Then he clicked his fingers, and another policeman came over to direct them to one of the smaller tents far off to the side of the base.

"Come on then, Serena, let's discuss our business."

Serena nodded, "Yes, business." Then, like a serial killer in a movie, she licked her lips.

They walked side by side. "I would remind you," Michael whispered, "you were only arrested a few days ago. Try not to act foolishly."

"I'll do my ever darndest, sir!" Serena whispered back, grinning at him. She made to take his hand, but he moved it away.

"You're my partner today, not my girlfriend," he said. "Try to behave."

"But tomorrow?" her eyes widened in delight.

Did I just call her my girlfriend? Michael thought. "Tomorrow, we're taking you to a doctor or a healer. Something is up with you."

Her nose twitched as they entered the tent. He shut the door as if that would make any difference to the noise.

Michael sat beside Serena and then held his hand out. "Knife, please."

"Why?" She touched her chest, looking positively affronted.

Michael cocked his head at her. "Serena," he said sternly.

She twitched her nose again, pushed up her glasses, and then took off the scabbard and blade, handing it over.

When he unsheathed it, he found it impressive. It was clearly expensive, full of brimming energy, and warm to the touch.

"So...what is it?" Michael asked.

Serena crossed her arms. "Paralysis blade, infused with great spider venom. Anyone you stab will turn rigid, assuming they don't die first from the wound."

"This...could come in very handy. If we poison the mimic, Tommy's soul should be fine."

"That's why I brought it, to help. *Duh*. I thought we could paralyze him until we figured out what got into him. It sounds like you did all that without me, though. Surprisingly, you didn't need me to read the books to you as you stared at my body, getting no work done."

Michael squinted at her. She seemed to be her normal, sardonic self again. Then he saw the cut bruise on her lip. He scowled and touched the side of it. "You hurt yourself," he said.

Serena froze, and her eyes glazed over with lust.

"Gods, is that all you think about?" Michael scowled. "My nephew's in trouble."

"Oh, you're one to talk!"

"Well, I've had a little perspective. Tommy first, us later. Okay? I'm extremely embarrassed it could have been any other way."

"We had no idea this was him," Serena said. "Don't be so hard on yourself. I do that enough for the both of us."

She gave a little scoff, biting her lip.

"I'll have to help you with that," Michael said, slapping her hand away.

"Fix me," Serena replied. It didn't seem like a question or a demand, more of a necessity.

"Not sure I can or want to do that," Michael replied. "Maybe just send three texts at most, next time?"

"Did you read them?" Serena asked.

"I stopped around your butt hurting."

"Good," she replied. "Delete them all, please?"

"I will, as long as you promise we'll see some healer or something. I've known a few neurological conditions that might cause such...outbursts, and I'm sure there are others drow have that humans don't. Maybe they can help you? Give you a potion to level you out?"

Serena's lower lip trembled, and a wash of tears flooded her eyes. Suddenly, she launched for Michael in a hug, squeezing him so tight it hurt.

"Serena, you are very strong," Michael said, choking as she squeezed his ribs.

She released her tension and then looked up at him adoringly. "You really care for me, don't you? It's not just about my tits."

"Meh. Half and half."

She slapped his arm. "I don't want to be this crazy, you know."

"It would be dull if you weren't," Michael said, studying her. She seemed to have settled now, breathing calmly. "Is there some like, drow thing going on where you can't be apart from me?"

She bit her lip. "No."

"Oh, that's a shame." Michael was hoping there was an affliction to cure, and she would only be crazy if she was away from him. Seemed to be the case anyway, but not from her species. That sounded more like a goblin thing.

"There's some *Serena* thing where I can't be apart from you," Serena confirmed.

Michael shouldn't have felt a soaring heart at that. He should have wanted to run a mile to be with someone more balanced. Yet, he couldn't help but feel touched.

"There's really no-one else like you, is there?" he said.

"If I've a mental illness, you're the only cure I need." Suddenly, Serena winced like she'd been stabbed. "That was so damn gross. I can't believe I said that. If you tell anyone, I'll kill you."

"I don't believe that for a second."

She hugged him again, gripping tightly like she was scared. If she let go he might go away from her.

Michael kissed her hair and took a long sniff of her lovely scent—as well as twitching his nose at the faint, sweaty scent of someone who'd just done a lot of exercise. He took another deep sniff, enjoying her natural odor.

"Patrick says you're fired, by the way," Michael said. "But he also won't do the bad thing."

"That's a shame," she said sardonicly. "I wouldn't have had to pay rent in prison."

"We'll figure this out," Michael said. "Until then, you're stuck with me. Full time, twenty-four seven, a thousand years, Serena and Michael."

"That's not how the quote goes!" She scoffed. "Gods, you're so old."

"I'm younger than you!"

"Yes, but you have old-man brain. I bet you type with two single fingers like you're pecking the keys for seeds."

Michael laughed, admiring her messy black and white hair. "You are funny sometimes."

Serena beamed at him, stroked his hair, and nibbled on his earlobe.

"You're mine," she whispered, breath tickling his ear. Then, her voice turned sensually sinister. "*All mine.*"

Michael smiled, feeling wanted and loved in a way he wasn't sure he'd ever felt before.

"Mommy wants a creampie, Michael," Serena added.

"*And* you ruined it." Michael pushed her off. "You know I don't like the mommy stuff."

Serena grinned, and Michael knew she was only joking. She was far too submissive in bed to ever seriously say such things—he hoped.

CHAPTER NINETEEN

SERENA

Now near Michael again, Serena brimmed with fantastical energy. Endorphins, dopamine, whatever it was, flooded through her, electrifying her skin and making her insides warm like a freshly baked hot cross bun, but in a very perverted way.

They paced through the police camp, and Serena wondered why nothing had happened. Michael was antsy and nervous, and she didn't like that. She wondered if there was anything she could do—apart from taking him to some alleyway and getting on her knees. He needed that virile energy for the fight to come, anyway.

And then he needed it for after.

Serena was being good, though. She'd hardly snapped at him—well, only a little. And she'd maintained her composure amongst the police, looking contemplative, like she was doing some very difficult math. *Six times nine something something pi.*

What was going on with her? Was she in heat or something? *No, I'm not some sex-crazed goblin,* she thought, *don't be silly.*

I am totally crazy, though. That's for sure.

"Maybe it fears all the people?" Serena suggested, trying to distract herself.

Michael nodded. "It's kept to the shadows before, striking in secret."

The wizard she now knew as Alabaster appeared, his silly uniform making him look like an AI generation.

"How goes the chest?" Michael asked.

The wizard sighed, shoulders fallen in defeat. "To all appearances, empty. I've never heard of this happening to a mimic and would be quite interested to discover how." He looked at Michael with disgust, which made Serena's eyes go pinprick. She actually felt it, a festering rage ready to unleash upon the man.

"As I said," Michael began, "my source could find nothing in there but the answer we already know. Still, the pages are nearly finished being photographed. What's your email?"

The wizard got out his phone and read it out aloud. "*Alabasterthemaster@manamail.com.*"

"How professional," Serena muttered, rewarded by his raised eyebrows, and she smiled wickedly at him.

The wizard shivered. "I await your email. Back to the dungeon I go."

Michael then looked at Serena, and they both rolled their eyes. "*Wizards*," they said in unison, smirked, then straightened their expressions because it was inappropriate.

We are so in sync, Serena thought in elation. *Like two beings becoming one. I want you inside me!*

"I'm sorry I ran off," she said. "When we were at the—"

Michael raised his hand, and it stilled her like her tongue had been ripped out.

"Totally understandable," he said. "I wasn't pleased to be around him either. I haven't spent much time with him in the past five years, you know, and only in passing. Seems like he's turned into a real git."

Serene nodded.

"But he wants to save Tommy," Michael continued, "and he holds the answers to that, so we'll have to work with him for now."

"And then, after?"

"I won't work with him anymore. I'll figure something out."

She watched him finger the badge on his belt, which was now uncovered. And as he fingered the badge, she wished he were fingering her. Her insides warmed at the thought. She felt a heat between her legs, like a muffin swelling in the oven. *You've already made that comparison,* she told herself. *Yes, but you could drip jizzy cream over it! That'd make a suggestive image.*

"You'll be too busy fixing me," Serena said, taking a breath to cool herself.

"Stop it," Michael replied. "You're not a computer part."

"Bleep bloop," Serena said, then grinned at him, then she huffed.

"Bored?" he asked.

"A little," Serena admitted. She swished back a strand of hair, then took her glasses off and rubbed them with the sleeve of her sweater, all while being watched by him. She felt his gaze travel over her. Even in jeans and a baggy sweater, he was obsessed with her body.

"I wish we were back at the shop," Serena said. "Before, though. When he wasn't there. It was just me and you, and you wouldn't stop annoying me."

"I did not annoy you," Michael replied. "I was just normal, and you got annoyed by everything."

"That's because *everything* is annoying. How could you not be annoyed all the time?"

Michael shrugged, inching a little closer, then shaking his head. He motioned for her to follow, and they walked over to the tape.

She didn't know where he was leading her, but she was all too happy to follow—*perhaps to a secluded alleyway?*

"What's the point in being annoyed?" Michael

asked. "You could meet things with positivity, or you could be moody all the time. One of those things is better for everyone."

"Easy for you to say."

"*Easier*, not easy. Even easier now."

"Unf." Serena gently punched his arm. "Cheeseball. Have you spoken to Orla?"

"I told her there was a way to save him, and I'm working on it."

"That's all you said?" Serena scowled at him.

They walked down the street to a coffee shop, which was thankfully quite empty but for a few customers. Serena needed a break from other people.

"Nice of you to care about Orla," Michael said. "What about Wilson?"

"Who cares about Wilson? Orla is my new friend." Serena stared at Michael, biting her lip. "She doesn't know it yet, but we're going to spend a lot of time with each other, and she's going to tell me everything about you. When you were a zitty teenager, what your first girlfriend was like, how ugly she was, and how I'm so much hotter. She's gonna tell me all the things you've said about me. I will *make* her."

Michael stopped and closed his eyes. "Orla is normal," he said. "She and Wilson aren't quite as prepared for your...*youness* as I am."

But Serena's eyes had gone wide, staring up at her godlike man. "They will embrace me like the sun!" she cried, making a few people in the coffee shop look up in surprise. Electricity ran through her. She brimmed with it. Couldn't Michael see? It was fate. "Or they'll regret it," she added, crossing her arms and scowling.

Michael looked worried. He was likely worried Serena would be best friends with Orla, and he might get left behind.

He didn't need to worry about such a thing. Friends were nice, but Michael *belonged* to her.

I mean, I belong to him, she thought. *I'm his princess. Yes. I'm his good girl. His big titty goth gf, and he can have me whenever he wants.*

He better have me. If he wanted me right now in the middle of the street, he—

"Serena?" Michael said, grabbing her arms. "You alright in there?"

She shook her head. "Fine, why?" she asked, then she grinned her sparkling whites. There was a little blood on her teeth where she'd bit her cheek.

It hurt.

~

MICHAEL

Michael smiled at the pretty drow. *That's right, nothing's wrong. Everything's fine and dandy.*

What could he do? Could he put her in a ward? That would be extremely bad for her. She might come in handy in the fight—maybe too handy. What if she tried to kill the mimic to save Michael?

Patrick would have some tools to keep her under lock and key until this Tommy business was over, but Michael wouldn't do that to her. Crazy or not, she didn't deserve to be around Patrick for another single second.

Michael needed to help her, not punish her. He knew that. Regardless of what she said or did, she needed help, mostly from herself.

And while doing that, he had to make sure she didn't hurt anyone. She was fingering the knife behind her back, stroking the handle seductively, no doubt thinking about how she'd stab anyone who looked at him funny.

The cashier was kinda cute, and he hoped she didn't smile too brightly at him.

"Two coffees," Michael said bluntly, sounding as pissed off as he could so that the cashier wouldn't be so polite, then Serena wouldn't see it as a threat. "Just warm steamed milk. Got anything like that?"

"How about a *vulta mentai creamblast*?" the cashier sang.

In the corner of Michael's eye, Serena's hand wrapped around the handle.

"That sounds great!" Michael said, grabbing Serena's wrist. "Two mediums please."

"That's what I said. Mentai!"

Now, it was Michael who wanted to murder her.

"Sure, whatever," he said, and, after paying, took Serena over to the edge of the counter.

"Behave," he whispered sternly.

"But she wants you to give her a creamblast!" Serena yelled, to the surprise of a few customers looking over. The cashier looked up and gave a sort of confused smile.

"I need you to be self-aware right now," Michael said. "You are acting in a way that you will regret, come tomorrow."

"You mean tomorrow I'll get to—"

"It's a perfectly normal word I should be able to use in a sentence without you filthying it up!"

She grinned, stroked his cheek, and pushed her lips out to kiss him. She tasted metallic, where she'd cut her lip on her teeth before. He frowned at it, protective instincts kicking in once more. "No more biting yourself," he said.

They waited for a while, and Michael held her hand, which seemed to satiate her somewhat. Then they took their coffees and sipped them, walking down the street.

Michael pulled his phone out, scowling at receiving no word from Patrick. "He said he'd ring by now." Michael found his contact and rang, taking another sip of the disgusting coffee.

"H-h-hello?" the voice stammered back.

Michael's heart stilled. "Just calling to see how you were getting on."

"Oh, just fine!" he said, so loud it hurt his ear. "Get your arse over here!"

"Well alright then, speak to you soon." Michael hung up.

"What's wrong, babe?" Serena asked. "You look all pale."

It hit Michael like a ton of bricks.

Tommy's great-uncle influenced Tommy to keep getting him goods. Dangerous goods Michael wouldn't. It was just the sort of thing Patrick would do. He could see that now.

And if the mimic couldn't reach Michael, he'd go to the next enemy on his list.

"Ready to perform a completely selfless act?" Michael asked, downing his mildly warm coffee. "This way, to my car."

On the way, he phoned Captain Vernon and told him to transport—under top security—the mimic's chest to the address provided. He also asked they not blare the sirens, and come in a subtle black van.

∼

Michael parked the car, then he waited patiently for the police cars in the rearview mirror.

Soon enough, one appeared, then another.

Serena crossed her arms, twitched her nose in frustration, and pushed her glasses up. "It would be a shame if I missed and the dagger hit the wrong guy."

Ah, grumpy Serena is back.

"All we're focusing on is saving Tommy. He's innocent in all this. Worry about your grudges later."

"Fine."

They left the car and approached *Relics of Wonder*. The lights glowed inside, barely breaking through the busy shop window. The police captain would no doubt make the connection that this was Michael's source. Patrick alive and in prison was better than being dead—if he'd somehow managed to survive so far.

And what about me, Michael wondered. *When they see that sword, will I be charged with aiding and abetting?*

He hoped the captain's ambition was greater than his sense of justice.

Michael gingerly pushed the door open, just to the edge of where the bell would ding, and when he slid himself through it, the door pushed against the rope of the dinger, just tickling shy of the rim of the bell.

Beady spikes of sweat scraped down the back of Michael's neck. He glanced in his periphery, hoping Serena's massive behind and tits weren't going to push the door further than he did. He quickly reached up and grasped the bell in his hand just as she was pushing it to the edge. If he hadn't, the force back would've sent it dinging.

Nodding at each other, they crept along the rows of goods, past glimmering potions, shining blades, and helmets staring threats at them. A dim orange light draped it all, and Michael's eyes stung with the effects of the caffeine, mixing with adrenaline surging through him.

When they got to the counter, he almost sighed in relief. Patrick had hung the noisy beads back up. Now, they crept under the counter flap and through the hallway, and Michael made sure to walk on the edges of the floorboards, where they'd be less creaky.

Miraculously, Serena wasn't making a sound. She seemed to follow his movements, watching where and how he stepped. This gave him a little hope that she was still in there, that her mood swings were just an extension of her emotions, not some madness that'd have her locked up.

His gun at his hip, holstered and ready to go, he crept along the wall and, aiming the gun, threw his whole body into the office, where the door was shut, and a very solid, gray-mixed creature dripped oily black blood onto the ground. How hadn't they seen it on the way in? It must've only bled it when in physical form.

It turned, and the frightening, youthful grin of Tommy stared back at him.

"Did he tell you how to get past this?" he asked. "I can't figure it out."

Michael fired a shot at his thigh, the crashing bang deafening his ears.

The mimic's body turned to smoke, and the bullet went right through to make a hole in the wall. It launched for him just as he was cocking another shot.

Michael spun and grabbed the chair, throwing it at him. The smoke dissipated as the chair crashed through it. This was enough time for Michael to cock another useless shot, knowing the creature had wizened to how to defend against his weapon.

Returning to the other side of the desk, the form turned into Tommy again, grinning wildly.

"You all let me down," it said. "My parents should've known better. I thought they were cool, letting me do what I wanted. What sort of parents would let this happen?"

Michael just breathed heavily, waiting for his moment.

"You abandoned me. Uncle Patrick took me under his rotten wing. You let that happen!"

"Have you considered just working the counter?" Michael asked. "A position's become available."

"Huh?"

Michael fired the gun. The bullet pierced his arm, then the door, rewarded by a piercing scream on the other side.

"Sandra!" Patrick cried, muffled through the wall.

Who the hells is Sandra? Michael thought as Tommy let out a gurgling groan, falling behind the desk. Serena pushed past Michael and leaped over the desk, screeching unintelligible words.

There was a crash and then a gurgled yelp.

Michael ran over to see her kneeling over him.

Blade stabbed securely in his shoulder. Not a fatal place, but a debilitating one.

The eyes froze, the whole body turned rigid, and Serena's shoulders relaxed too.

"See how easy things are when we work together?" she said, sheathing her blade as she brushed her hands. "Oi, dickhead," she said to the wall, "you can come out now!"

She grabbed Tommy and threw him over her shoulder, but Michael shook his head. "I'll take it."

The door began shaking and trembling, and suddenly, it opened up.

Patrick kneeled on the ground, cradling a mimic, its sloppy tongue fallen out, drool spilling too—no, not drool, some odd gelatin-like substance.

Oh yeah, that's Sandra, Michael realized. *Gross.*

"Don't just stand there, help her!" Patrick cried. "Do something! She's losing goo!"

Serena gawped at the sight. "Right, well, that's quite disgusting. We're gonna take—"

"Police! Hands up!"

Michael dropped his gun, Serena dropped the Tommy mimic, and Patrick just kneeled there before all the Knightseeker equipment and secret grimoires.

Several policemen ran in, including Captain Vernon, not far behind them. They all wore enchanted bulletproof vests. Alabaster was with them, too.

"It's all good," Michael said quickly. "The mimic's been put into stasis. It can't hurt anyone."

Captain Vernon squinted and whistled a secret command. Alabaster and his subordinates rushed around the desk, where Serena had unceremoniously dropped the Tommy-mimic.

"Checks out," Alabaster said. The policeman kept their guns on it.

"Thought I told you to wait outside!" Michael yelled, lowering his arms.

"You said to get here, not to wait here," Captain Vernon said. "And besides, I don't answer to criminals." He whistled. "Knew it was this place when I saw that sword outside. I swear, I've driven past here hundreds of times and always thought it looked an excellent fake. It's not fake, is it? It's the real deal!" He bounced on his feet in excitement, then cleared his throat and clicked his fingers. "Bring the chest in from the van," he said to one of his subordinates.

As the police dragged the Tommy-mimic out of the office, Captain Vernon strolled over to the gap, looking smugly at Patrick.

"And you," he continued, sheathing his gun and pulling at his vest. "What are we gonna do with you?"

"A salute would be appropriate," Patrick said through a sniffle, stroking his mimic's lid. "And a wizard to heal Sandra, please. Now!"

"Erm, yeah. We can do the latter. Until you tell me who you stole that knightseeker badge Michael was carrying from."

Patrick stood up to full height. "You see that?" he

spat through his tears, pulling the door open fully to reveal the knightseeker uniform. "This is the official headquarters of the Knightseekers. You're trespassing on noble land without a warrant! Are you going to steal our equipment, too? We've been keeping you safe for generations, and you want to stop that now? Just because we didn't see fit to fill you in on the importance of our duties!"

"W-w-well..." Captain Vernon stammered, clearly not knowing quite what to make of the situation.

Patrick hobbled forward. He nearly tripped up. "Captain Vernon," he said, squinting his badge. "I believe I see a promotion in your future."

CHAPTER
TWENTY

SERENA

Serena was very calm, and exceedingly normal. In fact, the flame that burned inside her was just a gentle candle, hardly even flickering.

It was not a burning fire as great as the sun.

And she wasn't about to explode.

During all this completely uneventful *not*-turmoil inside her, she studied Michael, looking up at him. He had that troubled, scowled look on his face he always had when something was bothering him.

At the hospital, they stood outside Tommy's room. Wilson and Orla were inside the room with the door closed, fussing over their son. As far as Serena had seen, the kid was shaken up by it all, would probably require some therapy, but then would be back on his feet, ready to put it all behind him.

And he would never raid a tomb or dungeon again.

The Walker—or Seeker—family were hardy. They looked death in the eye and shrugged, moving on. Perhaps there was some magic in their lineage, allowing them to remain stoic in the harshest of conditions.

Yet Michael didn't seem very stoic right now. He was frowning. What was bothering him? Serena dared not ask, in case she became unstable again. She knew that kept happening, but she suspected she was fine now. Totally fine, and would never go crazy again.

"Stop looking at me like that," Michael said, grumpy.

"Stop looking *like* that, and I will," Serena replied. "Now, hold my hand."

The smell of the hospital surrounded her—a faint mana scent mixed with the chemicals of potions. Michael took her hand, which fluttered her heart, and led her down to the waiting room, where they sat side by side.

"What's bothering you?" she asked. "You should be happy. Everything's worked out—except for Sandra. Gods bless her soul."

"Nothing," Michael said.

"Is it me?" Serena winced, prepared for the blowback where he would yell, *'Not everything is about you!'*

"Partially," Michael replied, putting his arm around her. "Though I've stuck a pin in that stuff for now."

"In exchange for what?"

He turned his lips to the side. *Ah, typical man,* she thought. *He doesn't want to say anything because it's about him and his feelings.*

"I won't think you weaker for speaking it," she said, running her fingers through his hair.

Michael nodded. "It's not about that," he said. He turned to face her, staring deeply into her eyes. She watched him gaze at her hair, tracing along the lines where black met white, then down to her eyes, ears, and lips. Feeling them dry, she licked them.

"He said what *I'd* said," Michael finally admitted, "to Captain Vernon, nearly word for word, and we'd not spoken to each other once to trade those lines."

"Well, you did work under him for a while, right? Did he train you?"

He said nothing, so Serena continued, "It doesn't mean you're him. You wanted to protect Tommy. Patrick just wanted to use him, then save him when it was too late. Same job, different man."

"I did let him be my assistant at the start, though."

"You're allowed to make mistakes. Do you think you're some omnipotent god or something?" *Yes, you're my god,* she thought. *You're my adonis. My Overpowered Stud Muffin 5000.*

"I'm not a Knightseeker," Michael said.

"What? Yes you are."

He laughed. "I didn't mean it like that. I don't want to be one. They take their children and train them to be heartless. Wilson got out and still couldn't help letting his kid follow a life like that. It's something in our blood, making us seek it. I think there's more to it than the training."

"Maybe you *should* be a Knightseeker, then," Serena said. "Help people instead of profiting from them."

"Here comes a rant about capitalism," Michael said with a roll of the eyes.

"I don't care about that stuff, not really. I just care about you."

He scoffed, but a smile remained. Serena liked it when she made him happy.

"You seem different now, *again*," Michael said.

"I'm holding it in," she replied.

"Anything I could do to help?"

"You know what you need to do. There's no fixing me. This is who I am. Can you handle it? My mood swings. My general moodiness, then what comes after?"

"I could certainly handle your moodiness. I think I've shown that already."

"You couldn't, I infuriated you."

He was silent. Was this it? Rational sense returning to him? Now the dust has settled, they were to part ways?

If you think you can leave me, she thought, *you're mistaken. You're mine. I have claimed you and—*

"Shut up," she said, putting her head in her hands.

He didn't respond to that. He just squeezed her tighter.

"I think it's a myth that people need to be the best version of themselves to deserve to be loved," he said. "We're already the worst versions, how could it get worse still? You said I can't fix you, but maybe we can fix each other just a little bit every day."

"What's wrong with you?" she said, looking up.

Michael just cocked his head at her. Then he stood up, rubbed his shoulder, and walked over to the window, looking at the happy family through it—broken, but slowly on the mend.

"One pact," Michael said. "Just one we need to promise each other."

"I'm listening." Serena's heart raced, batting against her chest. She was sweating. She needed to take her hoodie off, but she only wore a bra underneath.

"I don't want one yet. We've only been on one date. But, hypothetically, if I ever did have kids, I have to make them be a doctor, lawyer, or, gods, just a cashier. Not a tomb raider, and certainly not a Knightseeker."

Serena laughed. "Yes, because the best way to get a kid not to do something is to tell them they cannot do it."

"Well, promise me we'll try?"

"I promise nothing. What do you think I am? Some sweet bunnykin who will smother her oobi woobi boyfwend in kisses and cook his favorite meals every day? I am a drow—a proud drow."

He didn't look at her, continuing to look through the window of the door.

"I'll try, though," she added. "I'll try for you, you prick. You're the only person I'd ever want to change for."

"What if I don't like you when you change?"

"Good thing neither of us sees it happening then. I can live with you being the most annoying man in the realm. Maybe you can live with me."

He didn't respond.

"Are the police done with us?" Serena asked. She was feeling a little less worried now. She didn't really believe he would leave her. Her tits were too big, her ass too juicy, her feet too delicate.

Earlier, the police detectives had asked them to recount the event. Patrick was still in there, with a lot to answer for and a lot of threats to give back in response. As the lord of the Knightseekers, he held sway going back generations. It didn't matter he'd rejected the life. They didn't know that. They couldn't have. So much secrecy surrounded their order, which was, by necessity, instilled by prior kings to protect the future ones.

They were not the King's Knights with proud gems on their blades. They worked like traveling questers, helping those in need and secretly thwarting threats to the crown. The King at the time had felt the celebrity of his King's Knights got in the way of their duties, so when they were disbanded, thus the Knightseekers were born. Roaming guards, without unique uniforms—until they gained power and forged their own crest of course. Even changed their name to Seeker, to cement it as a lineal right, not a vocation. Ironic, considering generations later they changed it again to hide themselves.

That was as much as Michael had explained to Serena, anyway. It sounded like a total ego trip to Serena, but she wasn't going to argue. As long as it kept them safe and out of trouble, that was enough for her.

"They're done with us. We can go," Michael said.

"Will you take me home?" she asked.

"Yours or mine?"

"You don't have a home," she said.

"A little harsh."

"Would you like one?" she asked hopefully, then winced. They'd have to pick what to eat together, watch only shows both of them liked, and not use up all the hot water. They'd have to separate the chores and argue about who did what. They'd...have each other, and everything else could be worked out along the way.

"I never really like staying in one place for too long," Michael said.

"Oh."

Well, that solves that problem, Serena thought

bitterly. *It makes sense. We were in the heat of passion, going too fast. We're just slowing down now. It's normal. We're normal. I am totally normal.*

"I've always wanted to see the drow kingdom, though," Michael said. "I've heard the beer there can blow your socks off."

"I don't need beer to let you take my socks off, Michael."

He grinned at that. "So," he said, returning to sit beside her. "About that second date?"

She closed her eyes, the fire in her exploded as she took in his virile scent, and said, "If you don't take me to my apartment *right now*..."

"Alright, alright!"

She grasped his shirt. "My apartment. *Now*." She stared into his eyes and dared him to say otherwise.

"*Our* apartment?" he offered with a cheeky grin.

She rolled her eyes. Clearly, they still had work to do—that was obvious before and now even more. "About before," she said. "Where would you take me?"

"Which bit before? Where I'll take you on our date, or where I'd take you...you know."

"Yes," she replied.

"Oh golly, Serena!" Michael said in his nerd impression.

She shoved his arm. "Don't do that voice. Mommy hates it."

He held his hands up. "Okay, I'm never ever doing it again."

She grinned. "Fine. And I will never say the *m* word again."

Serena held her hand out, and they shook.

"See?" Michael said. "We're improving on ourselves already."

∼

MICHAEL

A man's voice rang from down the hall. "Michael Walker here?"

What now? Michael thought. He felt an inkling up his spine that the voice was different from the detectives' tone and personality.

"Check that for me, would you?" he asked Serena. "*Subtly*."

Serena nodded, lifting herself at his shoulder, then inched her head around the corner of the hospital ward, all while giving Michael a lovely view of her plump rump, close to bursting out of the confines of her tight black jeans.

"They look ordinary," Serena whispered. "Got these badges, though. Looks *very* official. Crests on them. Can't make out the details from here, but I think it's the Greenhaven flag?"

Michael held an idea of who they were. "It'd be a shame if we'd already left," he said, standing up and taking her hand.

They walked briskly down the busy hospital ward past clerics, doctors, nurses, and a few monks.

They gripped each other's fingers tight, and Serena ran a thumb along the back of his, comforting him.

Soon enough, the night city greeted them with cool air and blasting horns from cars driving through traffic.

"What do you think they wanted?" Serena asked. "To send me back to my realm?"

"I doubt it," Michael replied. "You helped save the city."

"Then what?"

"I don't care. They can just come and find us if they want to speak to us so badly. I'm not breaking the law by not being where they thought I'd be."

They continued their walk down the street, finally finding where his car was parked. As they got in, he put his hand on Serena's lovely thigh, and she cozied up on the seat, putting her feet on the edge, to which Michael swiped off. "Not with your boots on. I just got this cleaned." He turned the key in the ignition and asked, "Where do you live again?"

∼

Soon enough, they entered her apartment. Michael's heart raced as she yawned, lifting up her hoodie to reveal dimples in her lower back. Her lovely lilac flesh begged to be stroked, kissed and explored. Even that diamond slit between her jeans and top was enough to get him going.

Fortunately, the window became a little larger as she glanced back at him, grinned, and pulled up her hoody, revealing more supple flesh and the bra strap pulled tight against her skin.

Her glasses fell from her face, crashing to the ground.

"Oh no, my glasses!' she cried in an over-the-top pout, falling to the ground, fattening her butt out to a lovely swollen heart.

Michael stared, mouth drying and pants tightening with lust.

Serena quested for her spectacles, missing them completely, though Michael knew her eyesight wasn't *that* bad without them.

"Gods, this is uncomfortable," Serena said, pulling the dagger belt off and letting it fall to the floor. "I'm way too fat for these jeans," she said, pulling the button undone and letting the window open underneath her cute belly.

Michael tried not to laugh. She couldn't keep up the sex act for long enough to not insult herself. It only made him like her more.

He followed the half-drow down the hall as she kicked off her boots next, grunting as she fell on her side in her effort. Her body jiggled hypnotically.

"Bollocks," she said, ripping one boot off and then

the other. She flexed her toes at him, grinning as she rested her elbow on the floor.

"Taking a break?' Michael asked.

"I must smell awful," she replied. "A true test of your devotion."

Michael grew hungrier at the thought of it, and he walked over to help her up. Her boobs bounced in her transparent bra, the purple nipples mushed against the sheer fabric.

He cupped one, gently holding as they kissed, and her hand slipped over his jeans, teasing the nerves there to further entice him.

Serena pushed at his chest and led him to the bedroom. It was messy in there. A bottle of lube lay on the bed. He frowned but said nothing as she climbed onto it, making no effort to hide it as she placed it on the bedside cabinet.

She pushed her butt out, and the peach encompassed his vision like his eyes were a fisheye lens, everything around her buttocks becoming small and distant.

Somehow, Michael suspected she wanted him to remove her jeans. He may have to resist burying his face between her legs. They'd both been a bit active today. He could smell his own sweat. No matter, they could shower together later, perhaps.

Michael gripped the waist of her jeans and pulled with an almighty force, peeling the material over her juicy buttocks, pulling until he froze in shock.

"Why'd you stop?" she asked, twisting her neck to pout at him.

"That's been in there all this time?" he replied, mouth dry as the desert as he saw it.

"If I were you," she said, "I wouldn't take it out unless you were meaning to replace it with something."

"Got it."

Her jeans peeled further away from her buttocks; eventually, he yanked them down her thighs, calves, and ankles, unable to resist a little play with her feet. His thumb ran across her jewel-like toes, playing them like an instrument. She giggled, covering her mouth.

"I'm ticklish there," she said.

Michael then pushed her thighs apart a little to find the thong string barely covering the red, heart-shaped jewel lodged in her behind. He swallowed, wondering how best to continue, all while his cock rammed against his jeans, draining him of what good sense he had left. His heartbeat felt loud in his veins, and his body was hot.

There was something odd, though. At the north of the heart—where her butt cheeks had left a gap—were some metal spikes. It almost looked like the spikes continued all around the edge of the heart, digging into her skin.

When he grasped her cheeks, earning a lovely "Ooh" from her, he saw the red, deep marks in her flesh where the spikes had been pushing into her the whole time.

"Serena," he said, shocked, not quite knowing what to think.

"Yes?" she asked, pushing her butt out further to him.

"I can't let you wear this," he said.

"Let me? Who do you think you are?" She grinned at him. "My butthole, my choice."

Michael rolled his eyes. "Right, but—"

"You heard what I said." A wash of authority came over her, a snarl in her expression. "Don't take it out unless you mean to replace it with something else."

As much as conflict ran through him, another little perverted thought snaked through his mind—a worry he wouldn't have to face when entering *that* hole.

He nodded, swallowing. His mouth was dry as he grasped the bulb and gave a test pull. The flesh around her anus pulled with it, earning a yelp of pain from her, paired with rolled eyes of pleasure.

"It might be stuck in there," Serena cried through gritted teeth. "You'll have to yank it."

"I'm not doing that," he said.

She pouted, resting her head on the pillow.

Michael sat back, pulling his shirt off and then his jeans so he was just in his boxers. Finally, his aching erection was only confined by that loose cross-hatch pattern material, feeling much more free now.

"Right," he said. "Back to the matter at hand."

"Oh, you're oh so very official, darling," Serena mocked in a noble accent. "Pull away, Lord Seeker."

Michael scoffed, then reached over for the lubricant, pouring a little on the tips of his fingers. He pulled at the base of the plug, then, as her flesh pulled with it—"Oh, merciful gods," she moaned—he ran his fingers around her supple star, hoping some lube might get sucked inside and loosen the suction it so passionately gripped on the metal.

The entire time, he couldn't believe the circumstances he'd found himself in. He didn't complain one bit.

Michael wanted to find some sort of healing cream and rub it on the spikey red holes in her flesh. It didn't look cut, just deeply marked. He traced a finger down one of the rows, and she trembled, goose pimples flaring up her arms like a galaxy of stars.

Between her thighs, her slit glistened with sparkling desire.

"Wait," she said.

Michael froze as Serena turned around to face him, reached for the lubricant, and pulled down his boxers, freeing his red, hard sword from its fabric sheath. She pushed out a dollop from the jar, then slowly teased around it, making his silken head glisten, making sparks of pleasure shoot through his body, trembling his legs. "Now I'm ready," she said and turned back around again. "Take off my bra, please."

"Commanding me, are you?"

"I said please!" she pouted. "*Pwease?*"

"Don't do that voice."

"What you gonna do, spank me?" She grinned delightfully. "Oh, no, that would be *terrible*."

Michael flatted his hand and slapped it across her flesh, the ample lilac buttock jiggling as she trembled.

"Heheh," she giggled in delight. "Tell me I'm a bad girl."

He spanked her again, this time a little louder, the *wack* of flesh reverberating through the bedroom.

Michael finally grasped his fingers around the plug's base, held onto her dimpled lower back for support, and pulled.

"Guh," Serena groaned as the flesh pulled with it, then spread open as the bulb pulled through and came out with a satisfying closure of her star. It was a little red. She reached over and slapped it with her fingers, then gently patted it. Her legs trembled. Her toes curled.

"Babe..." she moaned. "Please."

Michael climbed over her prone body, grasping his raging hard cock and pushing the tip against the not-so-forbidden hole.

The very end rested there, ready to stretch her open once more. Michael shivered as he held it steady.

"Just one thing," he said.

"What!" she spat, making a fist and crashing it against the bed.

"If we do this, you have to be my girlfriend."

She snapped her head at him, a fire in her crimson eyes. "What are you, a teenager?"

"Oh, so you don't want to be?"

Serena turned around, wrapped her legs around Michael, and pulled him close, sliding a wet tongue into his mouth, sloppily kissing him with all the passion her words couldn't express.

He took this opportunity to reach behind her and undo her bra, and her heaving breasts drooped slightly from the relief. As she sighed from it, he cupped one, pinching the lovely purple nipple, bidding it hard.

"Don't you think we're moving a little fast?" she said, gazing into his eyes. She bit her lip, and he kissed her again, this time grasping her thighs and pushing them back. He grabbed his cock and pushed against her hole, spreading it more than the bulb ever could.

"Fuck!" she screamed, digging her nails into her arms. She clenched her teeth, and he felt her buttocks clench around his cock, making her wince even more.

"Too much?" Michael asked, worried he'd hurt her and struggling from how good her tight, clenching hole felt.

But she locked her feet around him, pulling him in with her drow strength. The tight ring of her anus clenched his nerve-ridden cock, sending waves of pleasure into his body, swelling around his navel, throbbing his cock with painful twitches.

Two tears streamed from each of Serena's cheeks.

She clenched her teeth and pushed her lower body up to him.

"Too much," she said, running her behind over his cock still. "So... stretched." She had stars in her eyes, twinkling from her pain and desire. "I can feel you where the spikes were pressing. It's...it's—great dark goddess, it's the greatest feeling I've ever felt." Serena rolled her eyes in disbelief. She looked like she'd taken some ecstatic drug. "And your cock feels good inside me too," she added, grinning delightfully.

She gave her pussy a little pat. The glistening arousal had spread around her thighs. Then she began rubbing, groaning as Michael pushed in and out of her.

He was beginning to understand her a little better, so he grabbed her wrist and moved it. When she tried to stroke herself with the other, he grabbed that too, and held them above her head.

'No," Michael said with a grin.

Serena nodded in passionate submission. "Okay," she said, a little more tears of happiness streaming down her cheeks. "I'm yours to do with as you wish."

He gave a thrust, watching her body jiggle mercilessly. She was so thick and curvy in her tits and thighs, her stomach so cute he wanted to bite it.

Serena put her legs above his shoulders, and when he thrust down, a wonderful *plap* sound echoed through the apartment.

He liked it. He slammed his groin into her again, submerging his entire cock inside her.

Her eyes rolled. She looked like she was being destroyed from the inside out. With a bite of her ear, she screamed in delight.

"Fuck me right now, and don't stop," she begged.

His cock was at the mercy of her squeezing, vice-like softness. Every push teased his nerves further. It felt like his cock was filling up with it, ready to release at the merest thrust.

"Yes..." Serena cried, biting his ear. He tasted salty wetness on her cheeks as her tears dripped to his lips. "Please..." she whimpered as he entered a routine like pounding, again and again and again. "Please don't stop." She squeezed him tighter. "Please don't ever let me out of your sight. Tie me up, collar me, drag me on all fours wherever you go."

Michael could hardly believe her words. He grabbed the choker at her neck.

She nodded. "I mean it. Don't think I don't mean it. Oh, gods, fuck!"

Michael was beginning to swell. Sweat glistened from his body.

Her ankles bashed against his ears as he squeezed her toes, pressing his thumbs into the soles of her feet.

He pushed his body upright, bringing her legs with him, while she grabbed onto her tits, squeezing her nipples with frightening force.

He thrust once, and a wash of pleasure came over him.

"Ooft!" Serena grunted.

A second time, it twisted and twirled around Michael's groin and cock. The scent of her pussy and elven body sweat wafted up his nostrils, making him feel a great warrior laying claim to his prize.

His third thrust, embedding deep inside Serena's tight buttocks, had his cock swell and surge so fiercely he felt it might explode. He was surprised it hadn't happened yet. Euphoria already blinded him, yet through that hazy vision, he saw the most beautiful woman he'd ever met—messy black and white hair, crimson eyes of evil, filled with love as they looked at him. Her full, lovely lips were no longer black but their natural purple. And her lovely lilac skin a perfect color. Her pointy ears pushed flat against the pillow.

Sliding through her a fraction of an inch, the dam broke. Michael swelled, eyes pulsing with euphoria, and an almighty yelp of surprise released from his mouth as he slammed down, right to the base of his cock, thrusting against the walls of her, crushing into her cheeks to push every last inch of himself into her, filling her forbidden hole with gallons of hot, oily cum.

"Fuck!" she screamed, her pussy quivering, begging for any kind of touch, but he'd grabbed her hands, mostly in an attempt to stabilize himself.

He fell beside her, his cock slipping out by mistake. He meant to keep it inside her from now until the end of time.

Serena cried out, "Guh!" Her body convulsed as

she patted her behind, trying to dispel the emerging soreness. "Gods damn, I feel like I've been skewered."

She lay on her front. Her cheeks spread for her hand, which she held onto her behind, while white cream dripped between her fingers.

"I suppose that's not the sort of thing you do for a one-night stand, then, is it?" She panted, gazing at Michael.

"We can still go on that second date," he replied, panting too. "Couples go on dates."

She threw her thigh over him, he put his arm under her, and he took a long scent of her sweat, perfume, hair, and their sex.

"I'd offer to...tend to you," Michael said. "but I'm damn exhausted. Give me a minute?"

"I can wait a little while. Don't worry," Serena replied, gazing into his eyes with worship. "After that, you're never getting rid of me."

CHAPTER
TWENTY-ONE

SERENA

"Cheers!" they all exclaimed, clinking glasses.

Her apartment had never been so full. She worried the neighbors might complain, but they hadn't about her and Michael's chaotic sex noises, so she doubted they would for this. Anyway, she was pretty sure they were all scared of her after all the yelling at the TV when she died fighting a boss.

Wilson and Orla, Calra and Clint, and, best of all, she and Michael filled the living room. The soundtrack from some indie game played in the background, it was the only music she thought appropriate. Only Calra would've appreciated her raging metal music.

Serena smiled, looking around at them all. Once upon a time, she would've put it on anyway. She still wanted to. This was *her* apartment, they were invading, and they should be subjected to whatever she wanted to listen to. If she visited Wilson and Orla's, they'd no doubt make her listen to awful stuffy jazz music that—

She took a breath and smiled at Michael, who looked particularly handsome today. Then, she checked everyone's glasses to see if their drinks needed filling up. Calra was sitting on Clint's thigh while she and Michael sat on the couch. Wilson and Orla had insisted they sit on some cushions on the floor. Serena had only half-heartedly protested, but they said it was the least they could do for her saving Tommy.

The topic soon turned to the prior days.

"So they still haven't found you?" Orla asked. "They seemed keen to track you down at the hospital."

"Obviously not keen enough," Serena said, turning her lip to the side in worry.

"Just think, the King's messengers," Wilson said with a whistle.

"Why'd they wanna find you?" Clint asked. "You in some kinda trouble?"

"Not according to what Patrick said when they came to speak to him," Wilson said. "He told them to piss off, apparently."

Serena stiffened at the mention of that name, causing Michael to put his arm around her.

"Patrick was asking after you, by the way," Wilson told her. "Said he owes you."

"He can shove his dick in a blender to replace that poor mimic he lost," Serena muttered.

"*Serena*," Calra warned and then shared a look with Michael, to which they both snorted.

"I think Serena's earned the right to say such things," Michael said.

"I won't judge you for it," Wilson said. "I just hope he's treating Tommy nicer."

"I think he's gonna be a lot nicer now regarding his employees," Michael said.

"That's two who've tried to kill him," Orla said, sipping her drink with a naughty expression in her eyes.

"Orla!" Wilson said. "You said you'd be sensitive to the situation."

Orla huffed, then suppressed a drunken belch. "I'm sick of being upset! It wasn't Tommy. He was trapped safely in that horrific little mimic's chest in the dungeons, so we don't need to feel bad about what that mimic did, okay? It had nothing to do with him!"

Serena felt Michael stiffen, knowing it did have a little to do with him. The mimic was acting on Tommy's emotions.

Still, everyone in the realm hated someone, it didn't mean they wanted to go and kill them. Serena was also furious that Orla managed to look beautiful even when trying not to burp. Serena wanted to chop her into tiny little pieces.

"It had nothing to do with Tommy," Serena

confirmed. "Hey, Orla..." She suddenly went quiet when she said this, and Michael rubbed her thigh.

"Hmm?" Orla looked up. She was ever so pretty.

"Calra and I are going out for drinks tomorrow. Wanna come?"

Orla smiled warmly, without the slightest hesitation Serena expected. "Sounds fun! You don't mind a night to yourself, do you, Wilson? Ooh, you boys can hang out, too!"

Serena saw Clint, Michael, *and* Wilson tense. It seemed that these things were more awkward for men.

"S'alright," Clint said. "I've got—"

"Plans?" Wilson said. "On lads night?" He shook his head. "Bullshit. If those three are gonna be plotting behind my back, we've got to meet them head-on."

Michael laughed, then pushed himself up. "Think the nachos have finished cooking."

"I'll help!" Serena said, a little too excited. She followed him into the kitchen, where the smell of melted cheese and salsa sent her to the heavens.

"I'm very good at this," Serena boasted. "I should entertain more often. Maybe start a video guide on how to do it."

Michael snorted. "Sure, sure."

She grinned, tiptoeing up to kiss him, then she grabbed his hands and placed them firmly on her buttocks, where they slipped under the purple skirt to grasp onto her fishnet-covered thighs.

"I'm trying to sort the food out," he said, squeezing her butt. She knew she had a *very* lovely butt, and every time he touched it, it grew ten times fatter and lovelier.

"Got your meal right here," Serena replied, and they giggled as she traced a finger on his t-shirt. He was wearing a pretend vintage t-shirt from a department store with a pseudo-faded graphic. She hated it. It was awful. Like something a poser would wear, which was a word she hadn't used in over fifteen years.

She decided it would look better on her bedroom floor. As would her skirt.

"Do you remember this outfit?" she asked, taking his hands and walking back a bit so he could inspect the skimpy corset, the fishnet top that rested over her bosom, the heart necklace, the choker, and the fishnet tights, too.

"It's what you wore when I first—"

"Fell for me?" Serena fluttered her eyelashes.

"Met you," Michael corrected.

Serena snarled. "Whatever." Then she pulled herself into him, resting her head on his chest. He played with her ears, tracing the points, and she came over all warm inside.

"Would you accept it?" she asked.

"Accept what?"

"You know what I mean."

She felt him tighten again. He kept growing tense

lately. This little thing eating at him would not disappear until he addressed it.

"Just because something's in your blood doesn't mean you have to let it become you," he said. "I think you know that all too well."

"The nachos are burning," she replied.

"Don't change a subject you started."

"Then don't promise me brutal bondage and give me a light little spank."

"It's only been a few days!"

"Ahem," Orla said, poking her head in through the doorway.

Serena felt a raging fire. She wanted to claw the beautiful woman's tendon from her neck. How dare she follow them without her husband? Did she wish to steal Michael from—

Serena swallowed. "We'll be there in a second," she said sweetly.

Orla smiled back, then gave Michael a lingering look before leaving the door frame.

Eyes wild in rage, Serena rushed forward, but Michael grabbed her wrist and pulled her back. "And what do you think you'll do when you get her?" he asked.

"Rip her fucking ankles off!"

Michael held both her wrists, closed them into her chest, and pulled her into a hug from behind. "Unfortunately," Michael said, "you can't make the drink date tomorrow."

"Why's that?"

"We're going on an expedition. A mission. A... holiday."

"This isn't about my revenge upon the mega slut Orla! You just don't want the king's messengers to catch up to you."

"Two things can be true," Michael said.

Suddenly, Calra popped her head in the door frame next.

"What is it, babe?" Serena asked, still clasped in Michael's iron grip.

Calra stared daggers into Serena. "We can hear everything!" she spat through gritted teeth. "Orla's about to flee out the window. Go and apologize *now*."

∼

MICHAEL

"This is...nice?" Michael said, a few days later, staring in disbelief at the tropical bar. Dusty fish netting hung on the wall, and the fake fish caught in it were thankfully made of plastic. "I can see why you told me to dress casually," he added.

"Here," Serene said, grabbing an oversized necklace of shells from a sticky-looking table and sliding it around his neck. "Now you fit right in."

Michael shook his head, admiring his drow beauty. She wore what she's called a 'ruffle top,' which apparently meant a see-through top with stripy black lines running down it, with some frilly black ruffles at the sleeves, elbows, and shoulders, hence the name.

Underneath, she basically wore a bra. Serena called it a cropped lace bustier. Michael called it a bra. Thankfully, the sheer ruffle top mostly hid any details of her body's curves.

Below, she wore a tartan-style skirt in black and thigh-high socks.

Michael knew better than to suggest to a woman —especially a woman like Serena—what she could and couldn't wear, and she'd been wearing stuff like this when he met her, so who was he to suddenly say she couldn't? Besides, she looked damn hot in it.

And he didn't exactly want her to start dressing like a cleric.

Still, she'd noticed his look when they were getting ready and said she'd only wear stuff like this when she was out with him or Calra, the terrifying orc. Not that Serena needed defending much, anyway.

Michael wondered why he'd suddenly started thinking about this stuff when he'd never even considered it before. He never got jealous. Never cared what Serena wore except to drool over it.

He knew why. It was because Serena kept worrying about *him* being with other women.

He took her hand, showing the entire weird empty bar that she was his, and traveled to the counter, past the oddest dancefloor he'd ever seen. There were lit-up squares of yellow, green, and other tropical colors, and the people dancing there were...quite odd, to say the least.

"I don't wanna get too drunk tonight," Michael said. We've got a long drive tomorrow."

"You best not drink a beer then," Serena replied.

"I can have *one* beer."

She raised her eyebrows. "Remember those texts you sent?"

"I had two then," Michael said, kissing her cheek. "Or was it three? I'd have to be totally wasted to want to text you."

"Very funny."

"Besides, how many did you have to want to send me a hundred?"

"Moving on!" Serena said quickly.

As tropical music rang out from the speakers—saucy lap steel guitars and plinky ukuleles—Michael thought she was correct. It wasn't so funny now. It never was.

How could he best say his thoughts that didn't come across as useless platitudes?

"Serena," he said, grasping both of her arms. She suddenly came over as submissive, closing her eyes, ready to devour his every word.

"Repeat after me," Michael said.

"After me," She repeated, smirking.

"Michael."

"Michael."

"Has no desire for other women, be they single floozies or married to his brother."

"*Floozies?*" she said. "What are you—"

"Repeat it!"

"I know you don't."

"Do you possess any desire for other men?"

"Are you joking?" She snapped her eyes open.

"Consider that, and flip it, then."

Her smile inverted in disgust. "Fine, when you put it like that. But it's not logical, and you're asking me to be! I feel it in my bones, Michael. My *soul*. You are *mine*." She hissed the last word like a vampire.

"So it *is* a drow thing?"

Serena frowned. Michael wanted to rub his thumb along her lovely black-painted lips, but he didn't want to smudge them, so he settled for a little fiddle with her ear.

Serena groaned. "It's territorial," she said.

"Like a goblin?"

I am *not* like a goblin." She prodded his chest.

"Maybe you're a drowblin?"

"Oh, don't be stupid, they don't exist."

"Are you sure? You know, I saw an elf with a fluffy tail once."

"Even more absurd."

"Sometimes, I think you like to refute things for the sake of arguing. Like, remember how you never believed in the King's Knights? Yet I constantly saw you reading that book about Juniper the Bard, who was—"

"She could be making it up!" Serena said, crossing her arms. "She is a bard, after all."

Serena pouted, then pushed her body against Michael and sensually kissed him. When she pulled back, she gazed into his eyes lovingly.

"What was that for?" Michael asked, taking her hand and leading her to the bar.

"Buying me another hour of time before you lose patience for good."

Michael rolled his eyes and waved to the bartender. "Beer, please," he said.

"And for the lady?" the bartender said, glancing at her and then away too quickly.

Michael squinted. The bartender was acting shifty. Had he tried to hit on Serena before and now felt awkward around Michael? He would meet the force of a thousand suns!

"Oh gods," Michael grumbled.

"What's that, babe?" Serena asked. "And a beer, please," she said.

"Not your usual?" the bartender asked.

As Serena snapped, "Did I stutter?" Michael snapped, "Did she stutter?" at exactly the same time.

The bartender fled and Michael swiveled his chair to face Serena.

"We got a lot of shit to work out," he said.

"Why can't we just have a happy ending?" Serena asked, resting her elbow on the table and huffing.

Michael tapped the sticky counter, pondering the best course of action. Logically, they should break up and both find someone who balanced the other out.

He took her hand, and as they stared into each other's eyes, he knew they were never going to do that.

"We could try meditation?" he suggested.

The bartender soon returned with the drinks, and they left the bar so they could find a nice table with some privacy. Or...

"Let's dance," Michael said.

"*Dance?* Are you joking?"

Instead of responding, Michael grabbed her hand, and they entered the dancefloor, past the shifty guy with the mustache and briefcase. Michael put a hand on Serena's hip, and she rested her arms over his shoulders.

They gently swayed, hardly dancing, yet not still.

"You're not going to break up with me," Serena said. It wasn't a question, a simple state of fact. "Even though you probably should," she added.

"You thought that too, huh?"

"It's sensible."

"We did say we'd try to improve each other."

"We're making each other worse."

Michael held his drink out. "Here's to making each other worse."

They clinked.

"I hope we get so bad," Serene began, "they have to exile us to some forbidden tower in the tundra somewhere, and we only have each other to keep warm and hunt food."

"Oddly specific," Michael said.

"I read a book about it once."

"A book?" Michael raised his eyebrows.

"Yes, a book. It wasn't erotica on *Twotpad*. It was a real book with pages and everything."

Michael laughed, and they embraced, feeling each other's warmth and feeling much calmer. He felt it, and he knew she felt it, too.

"I don't even care about any of that other stuff," Serena said, her voice vibrating into his chest. "You're not getting rid of me. Mine, mine, mine all *mine*." She pushed back and prodded his chest painfully. "Got it?"

Suddenly, Michael's stomach rumbled, and Serena bounced with excitement.

"Ooh, can we go and get food?" she asked.

"And get under the blankets and watch something terrible?" Michael suggested.

Serena's lower lip trembled, and Michael swore he saw tears forming in her eyes. She nodded. "Yes please." Then she hugged him again, and he could feel her smile. He stroked her lovely black and white hair.

CHAPTER
TWENTY-TWO

MICHAEL

On the plane, Serena rested on Michael's shoulder, snoring gently. Then she let out a little snort, and he chuckled, putting his arm around her and running his thumb over the soft fabric of her hoodie.

He was watching a video on his phone about 'Elven Ring,' trying to learn about the lore. Apparently, GRRRR Tolkerson wrote some of it. Regardless, it was nigh on incomprehensible—gods with way too similar names betraying one another for unexplained reasons that could only be theorized about by reading through the descriptions of random items you pick up.

But Serena liked it, so he was making an effort. Before she fell asleep, they'd shared headphones, watching his favorite film. She'd asked questions about it after, what he liked about it, what he would improve. Apparently, media consumption was important to Serena.

Michael stroked her hair and mused that it must have been her solace during her lonely times.

Serena snorted again, then licked her lips and mumbled something about snacks.

The plane was going to land soon.

Michael pondered on the reasons why he'd never visited Ilgath. You did not take drow artifacts, that much was obvious. They were a volatile lot, still adjusting to above-ground life after their underground origins.

Michael mused that he couldn't recall a single place he'd been that wasn't for the sheer purpose of raiding or seeking lost treasures. Regardless of all that, Ilgath wasn't exactly the sort of place one visited for a holiday. Recognizing that, Serena had insisted they could leave as soon as they wished.

Perhaps it would be awful, but the sooner they got home, the sooner they'd have to figure out what to do with themselves. So, Michael was happy for the temporary distraction.

∼

Serena was a little grumbly when they got off the plane, with faint lines of tiredness across her eyes as they trundled through the airport. She was happy to be directed by Michael as she weakly took his hand, her backpack hanging loosely. They'd packed light in case they had to make a quick exit.

The drow airport looked much the same as any human one, but the language on everything was incomprehensible to Michael. They also sold some interesting foods—a lot of mushroom goods where chocolate might have been. The drinks were brands he'd never even heard of. Fortunately, they still had McDerrels, and he wanted nothing more than a good old-fashioned...

"McMushroom burger?" Michael gawped, staring before the grumpy drow behind the counter.

"We're not the biggest meat eaters," Serena explained.

He pondered for a moment what such a thing would taste like.

Sure, at a human restaurant, he could imagine it tasting good. He'd dated a vegetarian once, and she'd made him bean burgers, and they weren't bad at all, regardless of what the most ardent meat lovers would have you believe. But something about McDerrels attempting it didn't instill him with confidence.

Something else had occurred to him that, of course, he wouldn't mention in a thousand years. Every drow he saw was svelte, slender, waifish even—except for some muscled ones. Even those bore muscles closer to a swimmer than a weightlifter.

Serena definitely got her curvy, luxurious attributes from her human side. Perhaps all the human meaty foods were what made her the perfect big titty goth GF. They seemed to eat like birds here, pecking at vegetables like it was a chore.

"One large McMushroom, please, with fries and a coffee," Michael asked. He wasn't going to turn his nose up at a new experience.

Serena got truffle-nuggets and fries, and they sat down and ate.

"Surprised you wanted to stop here, at the one thing you have back home," Serena said. "Don't you want to see the realm?"

Michael shrugged. "What would you have suggested?"

Serena sipped her cola. "Not a drow inn," she said. "I'd like you to survive at least the first night of the trip." She took another sip, her luxurious full lip moistening from the liquid. She licked them and said, "Not a restaurant, either. Half the food would turn your insides to mush, and the rest would just not agree with you. I still can't believe we're here, you know."

"So this was a good choice, then?" Michael smirked.

"Yes to McDerrels. Coming here? No."

"Why'd you follow me then?"

"What else would I do, sit at home and wonder about the many ways you're being skewered by *Ch'wanadas*? Or maybe getting tortured on a wheel of death? Or maybe eating some food your digestion isn't equipped to deal with. How's your burger, by the way?"

"Cooked to perfection," Michael replied, chewing the tough 'meat.'

"Really?"

"Sure, about five minutes before they stopped cooking it." Michael sipped the coffee. At least the coffee was good. The fries were exactly as they were back home, perhaps missing a little salt, but still good.

"I know why we're here," Serena said. "You want to see my tragic backstory."

"Or get advice from your father on what it's like to date a drow. He's here, isn't he? He's survived Ilgath. Surely, it can't all be that bad."

"I suppose not," Serena said. "There *is* a quiz on Thursdays at the local pub."

"Stealing my jokes now?"

"They're *our* jokes." Serena gave him an appalling look, contorting her face, making it look like it'd melted.

"So pretty," Michael said sarcastically.

Serena stuck her tongue out. "Being cringeworthy is fun. I can see the appeal."

They finished their food, got up, and left the airport, fingers interlocking as naturally as breathing.

Michael's nose twitched. The whole realm had a sort of mushroomy scent. Giant tree-size mushrooms of maroon cast shadows over the land. The houses were closer to medieval than modern, and there were lots of gardens outside growing herbs and, of course, mushrooms, though they were not without their modern conveniences. Cars littered the driveways, yet so did some mounts, too—odd creatures with six legs and mandibles.

"Are we walking?" Michael asked. "Or is that unsafe too?"

Serena scowled and took his arm. "It will be fine," she said.

"Of course it will be. You just want me close and depending on you. I'm sure this place isn't half as bad as you claim. Why, I could merely stroll up to this random house here and—"

"No!" she cried, gripping him tighter.

Michael grinned. Serena rolled her eyes.

"You're not funny," she said.

Some drow walked past, two men in battle gear, all leather spikes and whips. Michael wondered if they were heading to the local naughty club or just to the office for work. They sneered at Serena, not taking notice of Michael.

"You can live here if you are married to a drow," she said. "My father is fine, belonging to my mother."

Michael nodded. "I see."

"You are mine, yet my human desire to submit and

be yours is...stronger. Whether that's from living amongst humans, what was in me all along, or both, I don't know. It confuses me though."

"Could be worse," Michael said.

"Why?" she asked.

"You could be boring."

He put his arm around her for the whole drow kingdom to see, and because she did not protest, he assumed it was an acceptable thing to do.

She was soon given scowls by those walking past, clicked tongues, and some swore at her under her breath.

But when Michael looked at her, she was smiling.

"This is a land where drow claims what is theirs, becoming the leader or the follower in the relationship," she said.

"And yet you are happy for me to do so in public. Why? The rest of your people clearly do not approve of a human doing such a thing. For someone who cared about my well-being a moment ago, you seem not to care now."

"Nothing will happen to you," she said. "You have displayed your right to walk these streets. They don't see it as an insult, but rather a show of strength."

"But you?"

"They see me as the lowest of the low, one who submits to a smooth-eared short-lifer."

Michael stopped in the street and stared at her. "Why put yourself through that?"

"So you can see what you mean to me," she said. "Regardless of how we fight, this is what you are to me—more important than this entire stupid realm. I do not belong to them, I belong to you. If I give you trouble, you should not argue back, you should show me my place. Understand?"

Michael closed his eyes. "This is where the problem is. That kind of thing is all fun and games in the bedroom, but as a way to live? Day to day? I'd rather not be unkind to you by human definition."

"Do you think I am asking you to hurt me?" Serena asked, scowling at him.

"Then what?"

"I have told you many times! I have begged you for it!" She came closer and breathed into his ear, "Kinky shit. Bind me until I can't move, bent over so that I am presenting what you own. Why do I have to ask? Why can you not simply *do it*?"

Michael nodded. "I suppose I can meet you halfway on that if you're seriously telling me you'll be calmer if you get tied to the bed a few times a week. As long as you can promise me one thing, too."

"What's that?"

"That it won't always be like that."

"Oh, you want romance, tender gazes and slow, melodious fucking?"

Michael shrugged. "Belly to belly is pretty good sometimes, too." He laughed. "I'm a simple man. I like what I like."

Serena smiled. "You're right. That will be good sometimes, too."

"I gotta say," Michael said. "I did wonder if it was some drow thing."

"I told you it wasn't," Serena replied. "I'm fucking crazy, Michael. How have you not realized this? The other drow don't go off the handle like I do."

He put his arm around her, kissed her forehead, and stroked her ear while she made a weak fist at his chest. "It must be a human thing, then," Michael said.

"Or it's just a *Serena* thing."

∼

"By the gods," Michael exclaimed, stepping out of the way. A long-legged bug-like creature strolled past, seeming like it was floating in the street across the pavement, its giant body almost like a balloon animal in a parade fairground. A cage made of bony skin rested on his back, with several drow inside.

"The bus?" Michael asked.

"Simpler to maintain," Serena replied. "They eat the—"

"Mushrooms?"

"Yes. And they grow so quickly that they're more efficient than all the parts and oil required to run a bus."

"Must be a big mess to clean up in the streets sometimes?" Michael said.

Serena gently hit his arm. "It's this one," she said, leading him into the driveway of a rather middle-class-looking home, more like a manor than any tiny apartment he'd been in in the city.

"Suddenly, I can see the appeal of settling down," Michael said.

"Not here," Serena said.

"No, not here, but maybe out in the field of Greenhaven somewhere. Perhaps a small place like Peach Village? Or Moonmist Valley?"

"Are you trying to make me a housewife?" Serena asked. "Put me in a maid apron, make me bake cookies? Get fucked. You don't understand what I'm asking for at all."

"I understand," Michael said. "And you can wear that for *other* reasons."

She grinned. "Okay, that would be hot."

Suddenly, the door opened, and a drow who could have been confused for Serena's sister opened it. She was svelte and slender, practically half her size.

She stared daggers into Michael in a similar way to how Serena used to look at him, though this was...a little different, more menacing. He actually felt like he might be in some danger.

"Mother," Serena said. "This is the *gra'va*."

Serena's mother's crimson eyes turned to slits, not looking through Michael but cutting.

"Are you hungry?" she asked.

He noticed Serena tensed up.

"Depends," Michael replied. "Is it mushrooms?"

A flicker of a smile formed in her mother's mouth. "No. Serena's father is cooking tonight."

Michael's stomach rumbled for some familiar food. It was audible, and Serena's mother's mouth flickered into an even greater smile.

Then, her mother snapped at her and cocked her head. "You are looking skinny," she said.

Serena suddenly blossomed into a smile. "Really?"

"Yes. Keep it up."

Michael held his tongue at that, deducing just where some of Serena's issues came from.

It certainly wasn't from the kindly old man in the kitchen or the wonderful smell of...

"Is that spaghetti?" Michael asked.

"Spaghetti bolognese!" the man confirmed, giving a warm, friendly smile as he held his arms open to Serena, and she gave him the nicest hug.

"She is happy under you?" a silvery voice snaked down his ear, and Michael jumped as Serena's mother stood beside him, watching her father and her.

Michael hadn't even asked her name.

Happy, Michael pondered. Was that the right word? He could just lie, of course.

"She is," Michael said. "I do apologize. I never caught your name."

"Liar," Serena's mother said, turning to face him. They stared like they were about to duel.

"Happier," Michael corrected. "We're getting there," he said.

"*Hmmf.* Serena is never happy."

Growing up with you, I wonder why, Michael thought. *We've only just met, and you're unloading all your family issues on me. Not even a hello!*

"I'll take it from here," Michael said, standing taller. The slim drow wasn't very intimidating at all if he didn't stare *right* in the center of her pupils.

"Do a better job than me," Serena's mother replied.

He wished to sigh. Apparently, it was up to him to fix things, and what he needed didn't matter all that much.

But then he flicked a smile because he knew well, more than he knew much else, that he could express this to Serena, and she would do her best to meet him halfway.

Beyond everything, he was sure of that.

"It could be worse," he mused to himself as he left Serena's horrible mother and offered his hand to her father.

CHAPTER
TWENTY-THREE

SERENA

A few days later, on the plane back, Serena wasn't very tired. Yet she liked to close her eyes and rest on his shoulder. It felt peaceful. She didn't have to worry about anyone hitting on her or swearing at her.

Since meeting Michael, she felt like she'd hardly been given trouble for being a drow at all. Or maybe—she smiled—maybe she focused less on that stuff now.

Serena snuggled closer to him.

"We survived," she mumbled.

"You're talking in your sleep again," Michael replied.

"Very funny."

"Your dad seems nice." Michael put his arm around her.

"But not my mother?" Suddenly, Serena snapped

her eyes open to gaze at Michael. "You told me about your father. What about your mother?"

"Died when I was young," he said. "Very young," he added.

Serena squinted at him.

"Are you expecting to wring some tragic backstory out of me?" Michael said. "It's not that deep."

"Suppose you can't be traumatized by someone you don't remember," Serena said.

"That's one way to put it."

Serena shook her head, and then a brief smirk grew. "Remember when those guys challenged you to a drink off?"

"Serena, they were drow. I could have died." Michael sounded serious. He looked hurt, like he thought she didn't take his safety seriously.

She frowned and then snarled as his smile broke, because he wasn't upset at all! The bastard.

"No one would ever believe how you got out of that one," Serena said.

"Be sure to tell Clint and Calra so I look awesome," he said.

"They already think you're awesome. Besides, you really had to see it to believe it."

"Guess that one will be a story just for us then."

Serena yawned as they climbed off the plane. She yawned again as they strolled through the airport, her stomach grumbled at the cinnamon twists with the jizzy cream she wanted very badly, and then that made her think of Michael's jizzy cream upon her blueberry muffin and she couldn't wait to get home.

She yawned a third time, then felt something tingle down her spine because Michael had stood dead in the airport, looking at something.

A family walked past, obscuring what it was, but it was soon revealed to be two men with the Greenhaven badge on their person.

"Is it too late to run?" Serena asked.

"I don't think this is something I can run from."

Serena was grateful he didn't say something cheesy like, *'You can't run from your past.'*

Then she said it. "You can't run from your past, Michael."

"You'd give me so much crap if I said something like that."

"Yup!"

They approached the two men, two humans of about equal height with sharp haircuts and sharper suits.

"Michael Seeker?" the one on the left asked.

Michael nodded.

She got a closer look at their badges, rather, the words running along the bottom—*His Majesty's Service.*

She wanted to ask how often they had to service his majesty. Obviously, she did not.

"The King would like a meeting," one said.

"Patrick usually deals with this sort of thing," Michael replied.

"*Patrick,*" the man said, "has dealt with it. Now, as I said, the King would like a meeting and he's booked you in."

"Well, I'm bringing my girlfriend."

Serena tried not to snort. "His *partner*, actually," she corrected. "Like, his squire, not his *romantic* partner, though he is, but I mean his partner in crime—not crime, I mean, what the opposite of crime?"

All three men were looking at her in as much befuddlement as she deserved.

Say it say it say it say it.

She took a breath. "I'm his oobi woobi—"

Michael covered her mouth.

∽

"I won't dignify it by asking you what the hell that was," Michael said as they rode in the car.

Fortunately, they'd been given some privacy with a screen between them and the driver, so apparently, they weren't really in any sort of trouble. Though Serena held no doubt, they were still listening in on them.

"What I was trying to say was they'll have to hire both of us," Serena replied.

"Hire?"

"Don't play dumb. They're going to ask you to restart the Knightseekers. You're going to get knighted. Why else would you be meeting the King?"

"Not sure I deserve that," Michael said.

"And I don't deserve you, but you take what you're given and do your best to live up to it. Got it?"

"I thought I was supposed to be the dominant one," Michael said.

"Very funny. It's the solution to our problems, well, one of our problems, and—"

"Let's not jump the gun," Michael said. "We really have no idea what they want yet."

∼

All this was worth it to see the look on Michaels's face—pure bewilderment, especially at seeing his uncle Patrick in some fancy robe uniform.

Serena didn't even care that Patrick was there, in a position of power he did not deserve. She just looked at Michael's gawking face and stored it away in her memory so she could remember it and laugh with delight.

"I'm sorry," Michael said, "can you repeat that?"

"Told you," Serena muttered.

Their journey through the palace gates, peering

out at the grand trees and blossoming flowers through the tinted windows, had gone by in an instant.

She'd wanted to get out of the car and secretly admire the tall castle while making some snarky comment to show she didn't admire it. Maybe they could do so on the way back.

"I've hardly done enough to deserve the honor," Michael said.

"Modest, too," the King replied, glancing at Patrick and chuckling. "Not like his uncle."

The King was a man in his thirties, beginning to bald, beginning to pudge out, the benefits of youth finally leaving his body. Serena squinted at him and thought that he was just a man.

Yet, he would know if the King's Knights were real. She should ask him—no, she didn't want to know. Best let it remain a mystery.

She wondered very much how Patrick had gone from stealing the crown's property to standing beside him as a near equal.

"How's Tommy?" Serena asked Patrick.

"*Serena,*" Michael whispered.

The King batted his hand. "It's alright. She did save the city too."

Patrick just grinned menacingly. Serena supposed it might have been a friendly smile, but she knew it was menacing.

"Having some trouble with the cash register,"

Patrick said. "Perhaps you can come and give him a few pointers."

She took Michael's arm. "I'm a little busy with my —"

"Partner," Michael interrupted. "Any duties I must undertake must also be taken by her. *My King,*" he added quickly.

"*Never shit where you eat,*" the King mumbled under his breath, to a short scoff from Serena. "Fine, have at it. The Knightseekers shall be reinstated. You will get a holding to call your own."

"A holding?" Serena asked.

"A castle," the King said. "Presuming you can take the responsibility of quests, tracking far and wide at your King's command."

"At my king's paycheck," Michael said. "It's not the age of heroes anymore. We'll be taking this on as employment, not fielty. *My King,*" he added again.

Patrick's mouth twitched into a grin that Serena thought was pride.

"You won't be knighted for that," the King said, taking a deep breath of disdain, perhaps beginning to suspect he regretted it. "And you won't get the castle either."

"That's alright. I never like staying in one place for long."

CHAPTER
TWENTY-FOUR

SERENA

Later that day, they crashed into Serena's apartment like two tired hurricanes. Serena took the shower first, peeling her clothes from her sweaty body like it was stuck to her.

As she showered, running the soap over her body and feeling its softness make her clean and new and ready to be touched, she pondered whether Michael was making her food. She hoped so.

She ran her fingers down her abdomen, picturing his hands there, and thought that she had the food for him right here.

Her skin glistened from the shower water, a shiny lilac purple she was proud of. She was special, unlike anyone else. That's how Michael made her feel.

She wondered if he felt the same way. She

wondered—as her fingers gently pressed at her slit—what she could do to make him see how special *he* was.

Apparently, a knighthood wouldn't do it. How could they have stood before the King and treated him like any other man, like they had sway in the conversation?

That's how great he was, she thought, as she slipped through the slickening folds to her budding clit, begging to be touched. She drew her hand away. No, not yet. He should do it.

Then, she cleared her throat, felt herself go warm, and felt her legs turn to jelly as she continued to wash herself. She stepped out of the shower, pricking her ears for any sound that might alert her to what Michael was doing.

Serena yawned, dried herself off, and wrapped the towel around herself, not bothering to put on any clothes. She wanted to see his reaction. Perhaps he would rip it off.

Or maybe it would just fall off as she walked past him.

The apartment lights were dim now, and the sun set outside.

Putting on her glasses, the room came back into view. Serena looked at the posters in her living room, wondering if she'd miss them when she was on the road. Just what would they get up to? Would it be dangerous?

One thing was for sure: they hadn't seemed to argue as much. Was that because they had things to focus and work together on? If they were just in each other's company without a project, they fought. Yet another sign they weren't suited for each other, happily ignored by the both of them.

The universe was wrong. All the relationship books she'd never read were wrong. They were going to make it work, and there was nothing anyone could do about it.

Where had he gone, though? She yanked out her phone and saw nothing.

Serena shook her head and carried herself to the bed, where, on the way, her towel fell off, making her pout at him not being able to see it.

Then, she opened her wardrobe doors and found the skimpiest undergarments she could—a transparent bra with frilly black framing and flowers dotted around the transparent sheer.

Pointing her delicate toes into one gap, then the other, Serena lifted the garment up her legs and thighs, then pulled the thong between her buttcheeks, hiding that thin string between them, letting it ride between her cheeks in a lovely way she couldn't wait for it to be pulled back on.

She imagined herself bent over as he peeled it away. Then she put on her bra and began painting her fingers and toenails, flexing her toes as she ran the black varnish across each one, making them look like shiny jet jewels.

Serena sighed and then put on her makeup, too: some black lipstick and a powerful explosion of mascara.

Then she scowled, grabbed her phone, and decided to raise the hells.

That's if he would pick up. The phone rang, each noise stinging Serena's ear like it was stabbing it.

He did not pick up.

"Fuck!" she screamed, throwing her phone against the wall.

Suddenly, the screen lit up, and that awful sound started blasting.

Serena leaped off the bed and fell flat on her face—not before smashing her knee into the floor.

"Where the fuck are you!" she yelled, a few tears forming to ruin her freshly applied makeup.

"Thought I'd pop out to the shops," Michael replied. "I was a bit longer than I realized, but I got you wine, chocolate, erm, and several other things that would settle your fiery rage."

Serena snarled. Was that what he thought of her? A dragon to appease? How dare he! She should smite him where he stands.

"And why did you not text me to tell me this?" she asked incredibly calmly.

"I didn't think I'd be this long. I'll be back soon." He hung up.

Serena's eyes widened in rage. She'd gotten all dressed up for him in her sexiest lingerie, and this was how he repaid her? He didn't deserve her. He deserved to rot in the pit of the deepest dungeon where maggots ate at his eyes and ravens nibbled on his nob!

She stormed to her bedroom with no care of her downstairs neighbors, grabbed the longest, rattiest, oldest nightgown she could find, and threw it over herself, looping like a frightened maiden in some *olde* romance novel who carried around a candle holder as she inspected the noise in their mansion.

She threw herself into bed, pulling the covers over her head.

The covers were too short then, though, as they revealed her feet, and she huffed and kicked them back down, pushing the covers underneath her feet to make a protective barrier.

She lay there, seething with rage, trembling like a bomb ready to explode.

One text. One text was all he had to give her. He'd been perfectly happy to text her when he was trying to get in her pants, but now he was already in them, he suddenly thought himself better than to consider sending one, single, text.

The key rattled in the lock. Serena snarled and hid deeper under the covers. There was nothing he could bring, absolutely nothing that would absolve him of his crimes. No amount of chocolate or sweet treats or cinnamon buns with the jizzy cream would make her forgive him.

His footsteps creaked, stomping toward the bedroom.

"Serena?" he called.

Her heart leaped. She wished to run to him and...

No. Serena ignored it. The only way she could look on him would be to look at his dying corpse as maggots swam through his gelatin eyes and ravens pecked at his bloody nipple wounds and—

"*Treega, vellinto—*" a voice rang out.

"What are you doing?" Serena asked.

"Ssh," Michael said with a groan. "Now I have to start over."

"Start over what?"

"*Treega, vellinto, relanabto!*"

Serena's left wrist, where it had been huddled next to her right against her chest, was yanked back to the left of the bed like someone had grabbed it and pulled it. Her right thrust to the right of the bed, planting her body flat down against the bed.

Her left ankle did the same, thrusting out to the left corner of the bed and the right to the right.

Michael yanked the bedsheets from her, but before she could say anything, a magical mouth gag formed over her mouth and a blindfold over her eyes. And a sort of belt around her waist, pulling it up to force her butt to arch out in presentation.

"Like that?" he asked.

Serena tried to say, *'Yes, exactly like that.'* But all

that came out was muffled sounds as drool spilled underneath her magical gag. She opted to nod instead.

"Good," Micahel said.

In the dark void of her sight, she felt fingers tickle against the balls of her feet. She curled her toes as Michael tickled further. When she laughed, drool spilled from her mouth once more. It wetted her lips and cheeks, and she felt degraded by it.

In a good way.

Suddenly, a rip rang out as he pulled apart her ratty nightgown. She'd owned it for a decade. It'd taken him no force at all to tear it apart and reveal the slutty thong she wore beneath.

Serena pulled against the restraints and smiled when her wrist wouldn't move an inch.

It was a shame it wasn't real, though. Then she'd feel a pull against her skin, perhaps the rough feel of the fabric against it. Serena's ass pushing out was a total benefit, though, especially when he...

"Mmfmm!" she cried through the gag as the flat of his hand slapped against it. The *spank* sound echoed in her mind, traveling down her body, warming between her legs.

The second spank hit her other buttock, and she trembled and cried out.

His fingers ran through her hair, the tips massaging her scalp, and then they made a painful fist and pulled back, forcing her head back.

Just as he did this, he slammed his other hand down on her butt again, and again she cried out.

"Mmfhm!" Serena mumbled, through the sharp pain of the pull of hair.

Between her legs was as wet her pillow from her drool.

Looking out at the vast blackness obscuring her vision, her senses heightened as his fingers tickled down her back, clipping open her bra as it fell beside her, her bosom spilling out to either side of her.

He spanked her once more, and for the first time in days, she felt her mind empty, and still, through every painful hit, she calmed and became just a lovely toy for him to do with whatever he wished.

Unfortunately, she couldn't tell him this, and wasn't sure she'd be able to find the words much anyway.

She could only let out her little grunts through the magic gag. All she could do was swell between her legs, a burning heat so desperate to be satiated. Didn't he know it was calling out to him like it had a mind of its own?

Didn't he know that all he had to do was give her the gift of his cock, and she would do anything he ever wanted?

She tried to push her butt out more, but the construct kept her there, a little bouncy, not rigidly stuck, but still stuck all the same.

He let out a little chuckle.

"Trying to tell me something?"

She nodded.

"Unfortunately, this is the only time I get to shut you up, so I'm not gonna ruin that for myself."

Serena could not have been wetter.

"Unf," she grunted, trying to bite down on the gag, but it was more like it floated against her mouth, keeping her lips closed. It was its own torture.

She swallowed as, suddenly, his fingers slipped between her thighs, and he felt the soaked panties her thighs were currently smushing. That little gap between her thigh and pussy was pushed apart by his questing fingers, seeking the precious gem of her clit. And when he found it, electricity zapped through her body, signals of pleasure pouring through her.

Please fuck me, she begged in her mind. *Please just fuck me.*

He yanked the panties down, her sweaty buttcheeks clinging onto it through no effort of her own.

Her eyes opened wide against the darkness of her vision as suddenly, his nose pressed deep against her anus, and a tongue lapped against her clit. He kissed and licked, noisily wet sounds ringing through her ears as pleasure spun through her body like ribbons on fire.

Tongues and lips in chaotic passion batted against her sex, slicking her beyond what she could even produce. Spit spilled between her legs, her body tensioned, and she felt a submissive pleasure it felt like she'd been seeking all along.

"Unf!" she cried out so loudly through the gag it deafened her, as his face mushed into her behind, drooling into her, like some rabid beast, she felt every sensation of it tenfold. His fingers dug into her flesh, the scent of sex in the air, her wet sounds, the sounds of her grunting moans, the taste of her spit, pooling in her mouth and spilling onto the pillow.

She came.

Gods did she come.

Serena pulled so tightly at her magic restraints, her body tensing in its explosion of release. Michael licked and lapped at her, extending it beyond what should have been normal. For eons, pleasure swam through her body like a tidal wave.

More waves crashed upon her as it began to subside, extending the storm further. She trembled and quivered, her senses so jumbled that she could barely remember her own name.

Her face crashed to the pillow, her body twitching and shivering with little tingles, her pussy almost whimpering with incredible satisfaction.

There was a voice, some odd sounds not in the common tongue, and her restraints disappeared. The light blinded her eyes, and she croaked out, hearing her voice again without the muffle.

Her face planted the pillow.

It was very wet.

MICHAEL

"What are you doing?" Serena asked him, turning around.

Gods, her body looked beautiful, like some statue carved by an ancient artist, but this would be displayed in no museum; no, this was all for him.

"My turn," he said. "You got what you wanted, and now I'm getting what I want."

She didn't protest at that. No, she grinned and spread her legs, pulling Michael close; her warmth, both in temperament and actual heat, made Michael burn inside and out. He ripped his jeans off and shirt, too. It was a team effort, fiddling with buttons and then ripping it all off. His cock raged hard, almost painfully, desperate to be inside the embrace of her cunt that so desperately wanted it from him.

And it'd been withheld for long enough.

The tip of his silken head touched her entrance. The swelled red flesh met her purple slit, sliding back and forth against the glistened lilac skin.

She trembled below him, grasping his arms and staring with swollen pupils, barely even showing the red. Her lower lip trembled as she grasped his hair, stroking it tenderly. He just stared at her, all submissive, nipples hard upon her lovely fallen tits. It was like he'd broken her, though he'd hardly been rough at all; no, this was inside her mind.

He thought she was a liar. She didn't need whips and chains, she only *wanted* that. What she needed was him.

And he was more than willing to give it to her.

Without even a hand on his member, her slickened walls teased all his nerve endings with arousing comfort as he pushed through her. His legs buckled from how wet she was, sliding right in despite how grippingly tight she was. He felt her swell inside, ballooning around him to tease every last inch of him. Like sparks firing from fireworks, his body received signals of pleasure that increased and increased the further he pushed inside her.

"This time?" she asked with a pout. "Don't make me beg."

Michael closed his eyes. They were going to be traveling together, they were—fuck, it was hard to think. Every time he moved an inch, a mountain of pleasure surged through him.

He was about to become a Knightseeker, and she was included in that. How could she do that with a swollen belly? How could he do it without her?

But he also very badly wanted to come inside her, so, throwing caution to the wind, he thrust down, feeling her wet lips suction the base of him, feeling her juices slide down his balls and tickle them. He grasped her tits and watched them give, fattening in the gaps between his fingers. Her tongue stroked against his as they kissed and lapped at one another in a sordid display of passion.

Her body was so close to his, pressed tightly against his now he could no longer grasp her tits. She locked her legs around him, her arms, holding him so close the only part of him that could even move was his groin, and it methodically slid in and out of her.

He was glad he'd tended to her first. How was he supposed to last long in this haven between her legs? Hot, swollen desire slipped over his veiny cock and begged it for its release. How could he resist? It felt like what he was *made* for.

"Fuck..." she groaned. "Please...please just...please give me it. I need it."

He needed it, too. Gods, he needed it more than he'd ever needed anything in his life.

With a final thrust, he felt the swelling inside him, like the tunnel in his cock filled up with seed, ready to shoot, ready to fill her.

Pulling back a fraction of an inch gave another mountain of pleasure, and when he pushed down again, submerging right to the end of her, his eyes filled with angelic light. In that light, he saw her escaping from it like she was an angel.

Michael yelped, the involuntary sound making him as vulnerable as a kitten. Then he roared like a warrior, the great release being everything it'd built up to be.

He filled her with the warmth of his release, painting her walls and coating his cock, as he gave extra pushes, ramming into her, making her his.

Not that she never was.

They froze there in tranquil ecstasy, staring at one another in disbelief.

"Fuck," she said, closing her eyes and making a fist to bat against the bed. "Fuck," she repeated, smiling brightly, opening her eyes to show her euphoria-laden pupils, like black saucers in a tiny ring of red. She pushed herself up at him, hooking her legs again, and they fell on their sides, so they were facing each other on their sides, stroking each other's hair and staring at one another in disbelief.

"Worth it," she said, grinning and kissing him, her fingers delicately touching his cheek.

Her black and white hair, a little damp from sweat, was still soft to his touch. As he ran his fingers through it, she closed her eyes and brought her head closer. He stroked her ears, teasing the ridged edge, the point, running his thumbs under her earlobe.

Then, when Michael opened his eyes, he spotted the choker by the bedside table. He reached over, and she hugged him, seeming to think that was what he was doing; instead, he clipped it around her neck.

Then, Michael got up and left the room, and she whined, "Where are you going?"

He swiftly returned with the item from his bag—a leash, to which her eyes brightened, and gods did she look beautiful naked, his seed spilling from between her legs, where the blossomed purple slit was already glistening from his spit prior, and her own arousal.

He pulled a little at her choker to separate the ring from her neck and clipped it on the leash.

"Come," he said.

"You'll need to say more than that," she joked.

Getting up, he gave the leash a test pull, and she crawled on her knees, lovely fat tits falling and swaying in her movements. She crawled to the edge of the bed, gently guided by his pulling, then, with some effort, heaved herself down the bed, pushing her juicy butt to the sky.

Michael couldn't resist reaching over and giving her a spank, then a squeeze, the purple flesh jiggling wonderfully.

"Come on," he said, leading her off the bed finally, then she crawled to follow him as he took moments to watch her on her knees, curvy body beautiful and swaying, her tits looking heavy and hefty as she followed him.

"Where are we going?" she asked, her voice dripping with sensual obedience.

He didn't answer, leading her down the hall to the living room, where she continued to crawl as he sat on the couch and patted his thigh.

"Up," he said with a grin.

Dutifully, she climbed up the coach onto his lap,

where she cuddled into him, her butt pressing against his softened member.

He grabbed the remote, turned the TV on, and they spent the rest of the evening watching her favorite show, then his, then hers, all while tracing shapes on each other's bodies, fondling each other sometimes, and giving each other hand release.

By the end, the couch was a mess, but Serena didn't complain once.

EPILOGUE

SERENA

A dragon twirled around a glass tube big enough to hold a man. There were gems, glowing with their augments. Michael said that he'd captured half of them himself.

She watched him sigh as he looked around the museum and tried to understand his feelings. A time ago, she would've said, '*Serves you right.*' It wasn't even that long ago. How had he changed her?

He'd maintain he hadn't. Maybe he'd helped Serena change herself.

She held his arm and gave him a peck on the cheek.

A glass ceiling cast bolts of light across it like a galaxy of shooting stars. Glass windows held skeletons of monsters, some rare, and some common but too fearful for the average human to face. There were goblins, kobolds, in one window, the model of a phoenix, complete with faux flames, rose from the ashes.

At least, she thought it was a model. It would've been cruel to keep a creature like that in stasis. She shrugged, nothing to do with her.

"Did you get word of our first mission?" Serena asked.

Michael shook his head. "Apparently, the details are still being finalized."

"Just think," Serena said. "We'll be like the King's Knights—if they were real."

"Serena, we're at the unveiling of some of their swords! How could they not be real?"

"Could be a fake." She shrugged.

"I found it myself—forget it."

Serena grinned and kissed him again on the cheek. "They might write stories about us," she said. "That's if I even get to go. I might be stuck home with—" She patted her stomach.

"The burger you just ate? I'm sure there will be others." Michael put his arm around her. "Besides, we don't know. It was only that one time."

"It only takes one time."

"We'll just have to wait and see then," Michael said. "Deal with it when it comes."

"Would you mind?" Serena asked, studying him to see his reaction.

"The presentation's starting soon."

"Michael!"

He laughed. "No, I wouldn't mind. We'd figure it out."

"Would you prefer it later, though?"

He turned his lips to the side in thought, and Serena knew just what that meant. "Would be nice to set up some kind of stable future for the kid first. I can't deny that."

"Neither can I."

"If it did happen, we'd make it work."

Serena touched her stomach again. "We'd make it work," she agreed.

"We made us work, didn't we?"

"We barely did a thing!" Serena said. "Any moment, we're both about to explode in insults."

"Will we?"

"*Will we?*" she mimicked. "That's you. That's what you sound like."

She grabbed his hand, and their fingers slotted together as they left the hallway of creatures and entered the hall where a crowd was forming. Not one of them looked at Michael, though they should have. He was to be a Knightseeker.

The point was not to be recognizable, though. *And besides,* she thought, *these days, what is a knight to a popstar or video game streamer?*

Anyway, if he were recognizable, then he would have fans, and some of those fans would be women, and some of those women—

"Serena, you're hurting my arm."

"Hmm?" She looked at her grip, her nails digging into him.

"Sorry, babe," Serena said.

"What were you thinking about?" Michael asked.

"Murdering anyone who looks at you."

"Don't look at that elf with the white hair, then."

"What!" Serena snapped her eyes like an autofiring laser on target. There was a short elf with braided white hair and very long ears that went a little more outward than usual. She wore a white sort of gown draped in gold, and she was looking not at Michael but at *Serena*.

Serena blinked. "She sort of looks like..."

"An adorable potato?"

"You think she's..." Serena's entire vision turned red.

"I was just using your wording for her," Michael said. His voice was calm, he'd not been raising to her bluffs lately, and she'd always deflated because of it. Michael must've figured Serena out.

"Makes sense she'd be here," Michael said. "Considering."

"*Considering*?" Serena sang sweetly, tinged with venom.

"Are you feeling okay? I mean, you've read her book a thousand times and don't even care if she's standing right in front of you?"

Serena blinked. She blinked again.

Serena raised a hand and waved awkwardly to the tiny high elf. That potato of an elf strolled toward her so gracefully that it was more like she floated.

"She's coming over..." Serena said, gripping Michael's arm tighter. "She's coming over!" She shook his arm. Fear dashed through her body, and a cold sweat clung her sweater to her skin. Why was she wearing a sweater? Why hadn't she worn some glamorous elven robe of yesteryear? Or would that have made her like those guys who go to the eastern realm wearing robes the eastern realm hadn't even worn for hundreds of years?

"You're a half-drow," the beautiful, petite, white-haired elf said.

"The doctor says it's permanent," Serena squeaked.

The other elf cocked her head. She was beautiful, and cute too, because of her height—sort of like a corgi.

"I think that was a joke," Michael explained, peeling Serena's hand off his arm.

"It's not very common, is it?" the beautiful elf said. "I don't believe I've met very many."

"Are you...are you Juniper?" Serena asked.

The elf smiled, interlocking her hands. It felt like a practiced smile. Serena wasn't sure if there was any warmth in it, but she did feel it intended to portray warmth. Serena had read all about her and her attitude towards expression and...

"I know everything about you," Serena said, mouth refusing to stay shut.

"Quite unnerving," Juniper the Bard replied. "I suppose when you write it down, someone may actually read it."

Serena swallowed, urged herself to forget the last minute of conversation, and said, "My boyfriend—Michael, he's becoming a knight too. I mean, I know *you* weren't a knight, but you're...*ahem*."

Juniper smiled and looked at Michael.

Suddenly, Serena worried she might have to kill her if she dared to look at him again.

"Would you like some advice?" Juniper asked Michael. "I did learn a thing or two about the vocation."

"Sure," Michael said.

"Don't write a book about it. Everyone thinks they know everything about you when there is always more to the story. Keep some of it to yourself."

"I..." Serena said. *Oh fuck,* she thought. *I said the wrong thing before, didn't I?*

Then Juniper dug into a little pouch on her belt, pulled out her card, and handed it to Serena. "If you'd care to learn a little more, perhaps we might go for a drink together? Gerald was always saying I should make friends. I've never been very good at it, but I suppose a half-drow would possess some knowledge of the difficulties I've faced, or perhaps they may just emphasize, and I might learn about some of hers. Goodbye."

She walked away as soon as she had said goodbye, unceremoniously, as if she'd not been standing there at all.

Serena held the card, watching as the high elf made her way to the side of the stage, where the curtains and microphone were.

"Erm," Michael said. "Are you okay?"

"Do you think it will be hard?" Serena asked. "You know, with the age difference."

"You're only a few years older than me," Michael said.

"That's not what I meant. I'm going to outlive you."

"Most couples have one outliving the other. If you spend all your time thinking about the future, you miss out on the present."

"I should just say what I feel then," she said, looking at the card and pocketing it. "Because one day it might be too late."

Michael put his arm around her as Juniper began her presentation. She spoke about her past and the blades she would reveal to the audience. Serena wondered if Juniper knew Michael was responsible for them being missing all this time.

"What do you want to say then?" Michael asked.

"It'd be way too cheesy at this point," Serena said.

"I should say it when you're fucking me, and then it would go down a little easier."

"I think it would go down just fine. We've made it this far after saying some pretty awful and cheesy things to each other."

They stood silently momentarily as the swords—the emerald blade and the lapis lazuli—were revealed. There was also a lute and a crown. Serena couldn't believe she was seeing such legendary, barely believable artifacts. The King's Knights must've been real, she supposed, though she would never admit it to Michael.

"Do you know what I want to say?" Serena finally asked.

"If I'm right, it's something I want to say back."

She rested her head on his shoulder and smiled as he fiddled with her pointy ear.

"Do you want to get a takeaway tonight?" she asked.

"Sure," Michael replied.

"That wasn't what I wanted to say."

"I know." Michael smiled, looking down at Serena.

She reached up and stroked his earlobe.

The End.

***

Want to read another story like this? Check out A Tale

of Tail Brushing. (If clicking doesn't work, copy and paste the link into your browser.)
https://www.amazon.com/Tale-Tail-Brushing-Heartwarming-Thrusts-ebook/dp/B0CQ37VLV5

Patreon: https://www.patreon.com/kirkmason
Discord: https://discord.gg/jVeUnX4Juf

About the Author

Thank you so much for reading my story! It was written by a regular guy in his thirties, paying rent by tapping on a keyboard. When I'm not writing, I enjoy watching tv shows like Firefly, Freiren, and another one beginning with F. I jog to keep fit, and then ruin it at night by drinking Guinness. I fell in love with the genre for the way it lets men be men, leaving behind the worries and responsibilities of their life to experience something crazy and out of this world. But then again, sometimes it's enough just to chill out on the farm—because real life can be hectic, and you need to get a little cozy. Whatever the story, a review can make or break its success, especially at the beginning of its launch. That's why I'm asking you, if you enjoyed it, to leave an honest review. And please try to avoid mentioning spoilers.

Want to report a typo, or just need to reach me? kirkmasonbooks@gmail.com

Why not post a review of my book in one of these wonderful groups?

https://www.facebook.com/groups/haremlit
https://www.facebook.com/groups/HaremGamelit
https://www.facebook.com/groups/dukesofharem
https://www.facebook.com/groups/221378869062151

Printed in Great Britain
by Amazon